Prince

and the *Angels*

Also by Rachel Anderson

Letters from Heaven
Carly's Luck

RACHEL ANDERSON

Princess Jazz
and the *Angels*

Mammoth

*With thanks to the Khaira families in Glasgow, Scotland, and
in the village of Khaira Majja, India,
for all their support and hospitality. With thanks, too, to
Hannah Bradby and Gursinder Kaur
Khaira for advice and enthusiasm*

First published in Great Britain 1994
by William Heinemann Ltd
Published 1995 by Mammoth
an imprint of Egmont Children's Books Limited
239 Kensington High St, London W8 6SA

Reprinted 1996, 1997 (twice), 1998 (twice), 1999

ISBN 0 7497 2391 2

A CIP catalogue record for this title
is available from the British Library

Printed and bound in Great Britain
by Cox & Wyman Ltd, Reading, Berkshire

Contents

1

Up Above the Great Western Road

One morning when Jazz woke up, Bridie was not there. Bridie's bed on the far side of the high room was empty.

'Och, fegs!' thought Jazz. 'What's up with her today?' Not much got Bridie up out of the flat in the morning. 'I didna hear her leave. And it's no yet benefit day.'

At first, Jazz was annoyed. One of the few good things about Bridie was that she brewed a fine pot of tea first thing and took a mug to Jazz in bed. That was to make sure Jazz was up in time for school. After, Bridie was straight back to bed with her own mug, and staying right there till she could look the day in the eye, which was about the time Jazz was in again from school.

Now, no Bridie. No mug of hot sweet tea.

So Jazz would have to be up and into the cold kitchen to make it herself if she could be bothered.

Jazz looked around. There were few traces of Bridie. No cigarette burning on the draining-board. No dead fag-end either, stubbed out in a saucer of water, no shoes discarded on the hearth.

'That's grand!' thought Jazz, pretending to herself she was right pleased to be rid of her mother. If Bridie was not here nagging her, she could be back to bed and give over this getting-up-in-time-for-school dance.

So she was back to her bed and pretending to herself she was peacefully sleeping until the door chimes startled her.

It was a postman.

Bridie did not often receive mail, specially not small packages that must be signed for. Why must Bridie receive registered airmail from the people in India this one morning Jazz was on her own?

'Mrs Bridie O'Hare Singh?' asked the postman, looking doubtfully at Jazz in her Mickey Mouse pyjamas.

'Aye. That's me,' said Jazz, reaching out for the packet.

'It's a special delivery, hen. To be signed for.'

'Surely,' said Jazz, taking the form and writing Bridie's signature in a near-perfect forgery which even Bridie herself might be tricked by. Long ago, Jazz had discovered how useful it was to be able to sign her mother's signature when writing a sick-line for school.

'If anyone else calls, I'm not opening up,' said Jazz to the postman as she slammed the door of the flat after him and chucked the special-delivery packet on top of the pile of coats, magazines, and the old baby buggy, missing one wheel, which had been lying there since way before Billy Connolly was born.

A long while back, Bridie used to say the three-wheeled buggy was for the next wean, but after her dad Rajinder died, Jazz's hope of a wee sister went out of the window, though the broken buggy stayed.

She listened to the postie's feet trip-trapping away down the four flights of stone steps of the tenement close. She heard him reach the bottom and close the main door. She nodded with satisfaction and went back to her bed, taking Bridie's pink blanket as well as her own blue one.

After a while it stopped being so grand to be on her own.

Jazz was hungry.

She found a brown carrot, two potatoes, already sprouting eyes, and one tin of broth which she opened and drank, cold, straight from the tin. She was still hungry.

Or perhaps she was bored. Or lonely. Or annoyed with Bridie to be away without so much as a word about where, or how long. Sometimes a person had so many different feelings that they were all in a carfuffle so you could not tell which one it was.

At school, they would soon be sitting down in the bustling hall to a steaming plate of tatties and neeps, boiled mutton and pearl barley, followed by a bowl of pink rhubarb and yellow custard.

Jazz pulled her mother's blanket over her Mickey Mouse pyjamas, went down to the telephone kiosk on the corner and dialled 999. That would soon stir things up.

'Which service do you require?' said the voice.

'All of them,' said Jazz. 'And meals on wheels while you're about it.'

'Which service do you require?' said the voice again.

That was so like a grown-up, not to listen properly the first time.

'I already told you,' said Jazz.

'You have dialled the emergency number. If this is not an emergency, please replace the receiver so that others may use this service.'

'Ach, this *is* an emergency,' said Jazz. 'If you can no do something about it, I shall ring the evening paper and tell the people there instead.'

The voice went back into its parrot-speak. 'Which service do you require?'

Jazz took a breath and yelled into the telephone receiver.

'I require a rescue! Here is my description. I'm female. Ten years old. I'm wearing my Mickey Mouse pyjamas. I have curly brown hair, even longer than my friend Susheela's.'

This was a lie. Susheela had the longest hair in class. She could sit on hers even when it was braided.

'I have greenish almond-shaped eyes. And if you're still listening, I'm standing in a phone box on the Great Western Road just beyond the bridge. And I'll tell you for nothing, my feet are that cold for the person who shall be nameless, and who should be looking after me, will no buy me slippers. The clarty rat. Says I may wear my old trainers but I've left my trainers upstairs. I've been abandoned by her. My feet are that freezing. It is my guess, she has done a flit. For she is a

9

lazy useless besom who cares more for herself and her own black moods and miseries than she does for me.'

Jazz wondered if Bridie had gone back to her folks in Galway like she sometimes threatened she would if Jazz misbehaved one more time. But sure, she would not have left without Jazz?

If she has, Jazz thought, then I'll be really extra dead annoyed.

'Abandoned?' said the emergency services voice, abruptly changing from its parrot-tone.

'This is so. On my honour. And it is the second parent to do so. Now I have none left.'

'How long back, pet?'

It came to Jazz that perhaps Bridie hadn't done a flit at all, but had nipped down to fetch milk for their tea, and instead of going to Ahmed's All-Day Store just over the road, she'd gone on a whim all the way to the big supermarket. Once there, she'd noticed the cut-price things on the bargain shelf.

She'd done that once before, when they'd had a family-support worker called Monica. Monica had been telling Bridie how she must manage her money more sensibly. So Bridie bought the bashed tins of tomatoes, the smashed packets of shortcake, the bruised turnips, all as a way of saving money and pleasing the family-support worker. It turned out to be a fine way to lose money for both of them hated tinned tomatoes, the shortcake was that smashed it could only be eaten with a spoon, and the turnips smelled so bad they had to be thrown in the bucket. Bridie might just as well have saved her money to buy Jazz those slippers with smiling puppy faces on the front.

'I said, how long ago, dear?'

'How long, who?'

'When did you last see your mother?'

'Centuries back. So long I can no more remember. And I'm near to dying of hunger. Which is why I'm calling for your help.'

The emergency-services' voice became soft and sleekit like those teachers at school when they wanted something from you.

'So what would you like to eat, pet, if you could have anything you wanted?'

Jazz guessed that the voice had no more interest in her favourite food than Bridie had, but was gaining time. Then the call would be traced.

Jazz liked the thought of three squad cars being despatched and coming screaming down the high road towards the bridge, blue lights flickering and sirens screaming, to rescue her. But she didn't want to give the fire, police and ambulance services the satisfaction of finding her too easily by standing here. They should put some elbow into it.

They should also walk up the seventy-two steps, just like *she* had to every day of her life.

She gave her address to the voice, then quickly replaced the receiver and returned to the flat to wait. She knew she wouldn't have to wait long. Weans were not supposed to be left unattended for weeks and weeks, as Jazz felt she had been, though she knew it was probably not such an offence to fail to buy slippers with fluffy puppy faces on them.

For the benefit of the emergency services, she left the door to the flat on the sneck for she reckoned on Bridie being none too pleased, when and if she ever returned, to find her front door hacked to splinters by a frantic fireman's axe.

While she waited for her rescuers, Jazz turned down the sound on the telly in the kitchen. It had been flickering with life since before Jazz got up. Bridie always put it on, first thing, without thinking, as she put on the kettle for she said, 'Makes the flat feel snug, flower. And keeps us good company, all those happy folk blethering away.'

Now there was a schools programme. It was about foreign people, who lived in faraway places on the other side of the world, sitting under palm trees, doing their cooking out of

11

doors like they were camping.

'And though our lifestyles differ,' said the voice of the presenter, 'we must all share one world.'

'Another blethering footer!' Jazz shouted at the presenter on the screen, and surprised herself by letting the words come out as loudly as if she were yelling at Bridie.

She wondered what would happen if Bridie came back at the same time as the 999 people? Would it cause a right stushie? Would it mean certain farewell to any chance, ever, of puppy-faced slippers?

The telly screen cast its flickery lights right up the kitchen walls to the airer on the ceiling, making the damp clothes there all cold and blue.

Bridie was wrong as usual. Television never made the flat feel warm and snug. Warmth was the orange colours, red and golden brown like bracken, and burnished yellow like dandelions in the sun, well, that's what Mrs Macpherson had said in class one day.

Jazz moved the dirty dishes, climbed into the sink the better to look from the window. Peering eastwards, she could see towards Gallowgate in the centre of the city. Craning her neck the other way, to the west, she could see the distant hills of Kilpatrick. That's where Bridie must be, running about the open hills pretending she was back in Ireland.

She had done that one time before. It'd been Lammas so there'd been no school and Bridie had taken it in her head to go brambling. But she didn't just bramble. She ran around blethering about the brambles in Galway. It was so embarrassing. Jazz wanted to fall into a burn and drown herself. Jennie Stewart was there too. She just picked and picked and took no notice.

Bridie still said they must *always* look westwards from the kitchen window, towards those hills, because west was the direction of Ireland.

'Sure, Kilpatrick's not a patch on Galway. But it's the same kind of thing, all soft and green. And I'm telling you,

Jazz, that's the selfsame reason why they call that colour in the paint pots Galway green, because that's the living likeness of Galway in summertime. Sure, you remember the time we were there?'

Jazz remembered. It was like a video of summer in her head. But that was years back, even before Rajinder died. And maybe it had been changing in her memory, going mouldy just like bramble jelly forgotten at the back of the cupboard?

'And with wee Patrick? And our Moira and Tomas. Do you remember Tomas? Oh, what a high old time we had. And my Aunty Caitleen. Don't you just wish we could be there again?'

Jazz didn't listen once Bridie began her blethering.

'And another thing, Jazz, that I may tell you, there's no health in you looking always towards the east. For it's all hunger and dirty foreigners that way.'

How could Bridie be so sure if she'd never been there?

Jazz had once asked if Rajinder had been dirty, since he'd come from there.

'Dirty? He was so clean he near washed himself away. It was unhealthy, washing all the time, wasting all that water. Once a week, Friday nights, I said to him. That's what I did in my childhood. And that's what we do in this country. Not every day like you. Spendthrift, that man.'

So spendthrift had he been that he'd even wasted his own life by getting himself killed, and not yet seen the back of twenty-five years.

'So you'll not go keeking towards the east with those big eyes, do you understand?'

'Why must you run my life for me? So you're even telling me today which way I'm to look from the window? If that's the way you'll be, I shall no look from the window at all! Ever again. I shall run away to America and I shall get myself adopted by a lady who is rich enough to care. You'll see and you'll be that sorry you ever crossed me.'

13

Jazz had slammed the window down with a shudder and marched away to take shelter under her blue blanket.

Now, free of that eejit Bridie, she craned her neck still further out to look towards the east. Through the drizzling grey she thought she could just about make out the shape of the cathedral. Or maybe it was only an office block.

Her father had been a foreigner from the east. Bridie came from Ireland. But Jazz herself belonged right here. She was born, like half the kids in class, at the Queen Mother's Hospital which sat resplendent on its mound, lighted up by night and day as bright as a magic palace, getting new people into the world.

Her father was supposed to marry the bride his parents had chosen for him. But he'd gone away after a job and met Bridie instead. She'd come over from Ireland, looking for a job or trouble, whichever came first.

Jazz wondered what would have happened to her if he and Bridie hadn't each set out that Friday night and so had never met. Would she have been born as Bridie's girl, Irish through and through, or as Rajinder's all-Punjabi daughter, instead of as she was now, brown on the outside and white on the inside, like a half-baked bannock cake?

Or perhaps she would never have been born at all?

Jazz wished that people could send letters from heaven, or the Land o'the Leal or wherever it was they went. She wished that the little parcel could have come from Rajinder himself. She needed to get to know about him before it was too late. She could still remember him, but only just, and the certainty of the image was fading all the time.

At St Mungo's Road Primary School, they did not perform nativity plays at Christmas time as Bridie would have wished, on account of there being so many people whose parents might have been offended. It was, Jazz noticed, only the adults who liked to take offence about these things, never the children themselves. However, last Christmas, or perhaps it was the one before that, but certainly it was at least two winters after Rajinder died, the teacher, Mrs Macpherson, had read the Christmas story straight out of the Bible. And when she'd got to the bit about the wise men from the east, Jazz had felt all strange and excited, as though the world had stopped still.

She shot her hand up. 'Please, Mrs Macpherson, will you do that last bit again?' she said. 'Jamie's been nudging so I could no hear properly.'

'Behold, there came wise men from the east,' Mrs Macpherson read and again the world round Jazz was hushed. Jazz loved those words. She repeated them to herself. Wise men from the east. Men from the east. From the east.

That's where he was from. If only he had lived, he might have been one of the men in the story.

When Bridie, soon after, was in one of her rare chuckling moods, Jazz asked, 'Was he a wise man?'

'Who's that then, flower? Santa Claus?'

'No. Rajinder.'

'Was he wise? Don't make me die laughing. Course he was never wise. Would a wise man go against his parents' wishes and stick with me? Would a wise man go getting himself killed, would he now?'

So Jazz had not talked about it any more. But she had seen the pictures in the books at school of three wise men wearing brocade robes and richly coloured cloth around their heads.

Rajinder had worn a turban too.

Jazz remembered the long, long hair, smooth and shiny as black satin ribbons when he combed it out, but all day knotted up and secretly hidden beneath the turban.

Rajinder had been a Sikh and Sikhs must never cut their hair.

And now, there was no Rajinder and no Bridie either.

Jazz's rescuers were no carload of police officers, nor a fire engine full of firemen, nor an ambulance-load of paramedics, but two social workers. The dour-faced one waited at the bottom of the close in case Jazz did a plunk, and the other, grateful for the open door, crept stealthily across the sticky kitchen lino and grabbed Jazz down from the draining board, then held her fast so she couldn't get away. She feared that Jazz, in distress at her abandonment, might throw herself from the window down to the mucky middens four floors below.

Jazz had no intention of doing such a thing, not now when her life of freedom was just beginning.

And besides, she was that hungry.

2

A Parcel that Smelled of Spice

'There, there, Jaswinder dear,' said one of Jazz's rescuers in a soft sweetie voice. 'You're all right now.'

'I am not so. I am that hungry,' said Jazz. The second rescuer, with the dour face, hurried downstairs and returned with a steaming hot beefburger, plus double-extra chips, plus a thick milkshake, raspberry flavour.

'Raspberry, yuk!' said Jazz. 'Prefer chocolate.' But she was pleased. Bridie never bought her what she demanded. Bridie never bought her anything. She had never the bawbees handy in her purse, or so she said.

'Just look how she's scoffing that lot down!' one of the rescuers said to the other. 'The poor wean is half starved.'

'And what about the state of this place,' said the other. 'Just primitive. What do some people think they're up to?'

They seemed to be sorry for her, though Jazz couldn't see why. For a short while she was the centre of their attention. Jazz thought she liked it. She tried the asking trick again, this time whining that she was so bored she thought she'd go through the ceiling so would they tell her a story or buy her a comic.

But they were too busy to bother, both fussing round the flat trying to find clothes for Jazz to wear, and a few more to pack.

'You're going to be taken into care, dear,' said the older one of the rescuers, who told Jazz she was called Miss MacFadyen.

'Who's that then?' Jazz said.

'Not who, dear. Where. It means we'll be taking you to

stay with some really pleasant people who'll be looking after you.'

'Just for a wee while,' added the other one.

'They're a most kindly couple. I'm sure you'll get on like a house on fire, I mean very well.'

What they meant was they couldn't think what else to do with a carnaptious child in Mickey Mouse pyjamas, found sitting on a draining-board alone in a grubby tenement flat.

'You won't mind, will you?'

'Sounds grand to me. Anything for out of here.'

And anything to really fash Bridie, Jazz thought, when she gets back in and finds I've flown to America.

'Do you have any toilet things to bring with you?' one of the rescuers asked.

Jazz shrugged. 'I dunno.'

'Just your toothbrush, maybe?'

Jazz shrugged.

'Is there maybe a special toy you'd like to bring, dear?'

Jazz couldn't decide whether to say she was far too old for playthings, or to make her eyes big and sad and say she had never had any toys. It was indeed true that the only toy she had ever really loved was the coloured paper doll which had arrived one day in an envelope from Rajinder's people. Jazz used to stare into its demure painted face and wish it could talk and tell her about the place it had come from.

But, by mistake, Jazz had left it lying on the floor where Bridie had dropped a half-stubbed-out cigarette onto it. In next to no time, the doll had burned up into nothing, and a patch of the lino too.

While searching for one of Jazz's socks, to match the one which had already been found under the telly, Miss MacFadyen came across the special-delivery packet which Jazz had tossed away behind the door.

'Och!' said Jazz, pouncing for it. 'Mine!'

'No, dear. It's addressed to your mother.'

'And meant for me,' said Jazz, grabbing it back and

holding on tight as a bog leech.

She wondered what was inside. The packet was so thin it couldn't be anything big or worthwhile, probably not very interesting either. Even so, why should Bridie have it, whatever it was, when she was always so rude about Rajinder's folk?

Jazz said, 'That name, that's just a mistake they made. They got it wrong. They get us muddled. They can no write properly on account of them being foreigners.'

She pressed the packet to her face and breathed in deeply.

'That's India,' she said. She knew she could smell something foreign and faraway through the paper wrapping.

'I dare say, dear. But Mrs Bridie O'Hare Singh, is that not your mother's name?'

'She's not called Singh. Nobody calls her that. Do you not know anything. That was *his* name, never hers.'

It seemed to Jazz that, even though the Sikh people didn't celebrate Christmas, they just might have heard about it in their faraway village. As a way of being friendly to poor Bridie, they might have decided to send her a very early present. However, in Jazz's opinion, Bridie did not deserve any kind of present, not when she'd set fire to the paper doll.

'It's mine, mine,' she insisted now and held the packet so tightly that the two rescuers gave up trying to prise it from her hands.

Sure enough, as it later turned out, the packet was indeed meant for Jazz, though there was no paper doll inside.

Being in care was, Jazz found, worse than a wet Sunday. Each hour of each day was too long. The couple were orderly. They had no arguments. Their place was out of town, way beyond the spread of the city, towards Bearsden, where all the homes were in tidy rows. Each had a garden and each garden had a little gate. Jazz had not stayed in a house with a garden. Even over in Ireland with Bridie's people, although Jazz could dimly recall streams and meadows, hillsides and a mucky yard full of cows, she could not recall any garden like this, with its straight concrete path and its two tidy flowerbeds. As she quickly found, there was not a lot you could do with such a garden, except walk to the end of it and then walk back, after which you might as well come in again and watch television.

The foster couple did everything in a regular and orderly way, always got up at the same time, encouraged Jazz to help them feed their goldfish at the same time, washed up the dishes at the same time and in the same order, and always told Jazz the same anecdotes about the other foster girls and boys who had been sent to stay with them.

'Blether, blether, blether,' said Jazz, yawning with her mouth open wide.

She decided to ignore them. She pretended to herself that she was a princess and they were her servants. She spoke to them only when she wanted them to do something for her, like fetch her trainers from upstairs or ask if her mother had been in touch yet.

Jazz had a room of her own, with its own chest of drawers, its own wash-basin, its own tall wooden wardrobe full of padded coat hangers. She had never had a room of her own. She put Bridie's packet in the darkness at the bottom of the wardrobe, hidden behind the plastic supermarket bag which Miss MacFadyen had packed for her, where it could not be seen.

Before she went to sleep, she checked that it was still there.

It was. The foster woman didn't know about it. Only the two rescuers who had wanted to take it away from her knew about it and they hadn't seen her hide it.

Now she took it out and shook it, then squeezed it.

'Hello, my dear wee Punjabi parcel,' she thought inside her head, though her lips didn't move. She stared at the Indian stamps which had strange black writing on them, not like the writing here. She pushed her face into the packet and today she was sure she could smell a prickly sweet, peppery sweet, scent of ground spices. She returned the packet quickly to the back of the wardrobe.

'Night night, packet,' she whispered. 'God bless and sleep tight.'

That's what Bridie always used to say. 'God bless and sleep tight. Angels guard you till it's light.'

Next time when she went to take a quick keek, it was not so much the spiciness she noticed as she sniffed at the brown paper wrapping, as the smell of a red dusty road, then the sharpness of a freshly sliced green lime.

Those were the things she remembered, or thought she remembered, Rajinder telling her about his village when she was too young to understand. Or perhaps she had only imagined him ever telling her anything. Some days, she could not even remember what he looked like.

She placed the packet carefully back in its dim corner. It was like a secret friend, except that it never spoke, or answered back, or argued with her.

'God bless and sleep tight. Please do no be too lonely, all on your own, in the dark.'

She closed the wardrobe door.

There was just one good thing about staying with the boring couple. All the time Miss MacFadyen was busy deciding what to do about Jazz, nobody mentioned anything about St Mungo's or any other school. This was unusual. Normally, everybody was telling you how you had to go there, how you mustn't be late, how you had to work hard or you'd never get anywhere. Yet now Jazz was allowed to sit around all day doing nothing but watch the goldfish swimming round its tank.

Another long hour passed and grew into another long day. Jazz grew restless. Surely Bridie must come to find her soon? And if she was away off to Galway, why did she not send a picture postcard of those green hills she was always blethering on about?

How dare she ignore Jazz? Jazz would punish her. She would open the packet.

Jazz ran up to the bedroom, closed the door, scrabbled for the packet and tore into the wrapping.

Inside, she found some flimsy pink material, neatly folded, a ticket for an airline with a lot of printed writing on it, and a letter from one of Rajinder's people.

They'd written to Bridie before, each time asking when Bridie and Jaswinder were coming to visit. Bridie always threw the letters away. She did not want to go to the village.

'And nor do you,' she used to tell Jazz.

'Never said I did.'

'And if I'd not been such a eejit, I'd have married a white man, then none of this would have happened, and we wouldn't have been left on our uppers.'

'If none of what had happened?' Jazz used to want to ask. But when Bridie was in one of her black-dog miseries it was best to say nothing and crawl away under the blanket.

Rajinder had died because he was Asian. At least, that's what Bridie used to say. There'd been a fight near a pub. Nobody had actually killed him. He'd had a heart attack, right there in the commotion on the pavement outside *The Rubaiyat*.

'So the coroner would have it,' Bridie used to say. 'Either way, he's dead.'

This time, the letter did not enquire when they were coming. It merely stated that Rajneet Singh, whoever he was, would be at Mahatma Gandhi airport in New Delhi to meet Jaswinder Kaur off the plane.

Jazz stared at the careful curly script. Did Rajinder's people really want to see her so much they'd buy a ticket for her?

Jazz shook out the flimsy fabric and found three garments made of a material so fine that, folded flat, they took up no more space than a few sheets of airmail paper. The silk was the soft colour of the petals that fell, in late summer, from the tired rose bushes in Kelvin Park.

The pink silk fabric was a loose trim tunic top with a straight neckline and long sleeves down to the wrist, and a pair of broad gathered trousers with embroidered cuffs at the ankles. To go with them was a long *dupatta* scarf, all light and shimmery.

The outfit looked about the right size for a girl of ten years old and Jazz knew that these things were meant for her. Almost without thinking and quite against her intention, she tried them on. The silk felt soft and smooth, just as Jazz imagined warm air would feel against your skin on a still evening as the sun went down. If you lived way over in the east, beyond Gallowgate, did the sun still set in the west?

Bridie had once had a *salvar kameez* like this, not pink but scarlet, edged with golden tinsel, presented to her, along with a dozen golden bangles for her arms, when she'd married Rajinder in the Registery Office. After he'd died, she'd hidden everything away in the box under her bed. Jazz had never seen her wear the suit, nor the golden bangles.

Jazz draped the long scarf round her shoulders, like Susheela and Vidna did, then pulled it up over her head like Susheela's mother and grandmother and three aunties did. She looked at herself in the mirror. Even though her eyes were so green and her hair so curly, she looked amost Asian.

She placed the palms of her hands together, as if she were Bridie saying her prayers at Mass, and bowed to her reflection.

'Greetings, O fair princess,' she said to herself with a graceful bow.

Suddenly, without any warning, before Jazz had even time to pull down the scarf, the foster woman came in and saw her standing there all dressed up like a Punjabi girl.

'Why, what a bonny dress you have there,' she said.

'It's not a dress,' snapped Jazz. 'It's called a *salvar kameez*.' She hurriedly threw off the scarf, dragged the tunic top over her head, and struggled out of the gathered trousers.

23

'Such a pretty colour. It takes your skin tones well.'

'No it doesn't. Whoever wore pink? No one with any street cred, that's for sure. It's a really stupid naff colour. The colour for rhubarb. I never ever wear pink and I hate rhubarb.'

She flung the garments to the floor and pulled on her jeans. The foster woman picked up the offending garments, smoothed them, folded them neatly, and put them tidily away. Jazz stomped downstairs to lie on the chintz settee with her trainers on the cushions, pretending to be asleep.

Actually she was busy thinking. Knowing that Bridie wouldn't want her to go helped Jazz to make up her mind.

She let the foster woman find the letter for she knew she'd read it.

When Miss MacFadyen came to make her weekly call, Jazz let her talk.

'So it certainly could be a wonderful opportunity to meet the rest of your family, to find the other half of your identity, couldn't it?'

Jazz shrugged. 'Maybe. Except they're *not* my family. I'm from Glasgow, all my friends know it. You ask Jennie Stewart. She sits next to me at school. She knows who I am.'

Still, she let Miss MacFadyen talk her into it so that, in a half-hearted sort of way, Jazz agreed.

'Except I'll not be wearing that pink thing. No way.'

After that, everything except the activities of the goldfish began to speed up as the social workers took over organising Jazz's life.

'And we've managed to be in touch with your uncle,' said Miss MacFadyen.

'Uncle? What uncle?' Clearly, she didn't mean Bridie's younger brother in Ireland.

'Mr Singh, your uncle in India who sent you the pretty pink suit. He'll be there to meet you.'

'And I've told you before, if I have to go and see them, I will, but I'm no wearing the pink rubbish, no way.'

'And a counsellor's been helping your mother.'

'What's that supposed to mean?'

Does she want to see me? Please say she does, Jazz wanted to say.

'We don't feel she's quite ready to have you back. Not just yet. She'll need to get herself straight and receive help with her parenting skills.'

'Grand,' said Jazz. Bridie needed to be taught a few lessons.

When Bridie came to see Jazz it was called a supervised visit, which meant that Miss MacFadyen came too,

Bridie and Jazz sat in the tidy front room watching the goldfish move slowly round the tank. Miss MacFadyen sat looking at her hands. Bridie was pale and her make-up smudged.

'You're looking well, flower,' she said. 'They're taking care of you then?'

'And you're looking right peelie-wally!' said Jazz. 'You did a flit on me, didn't you?'

Bridie lit a cigarette.

'No! It's no permited here. They do no care for smoking here,' said Jazz. But the foster couple were out in their garden, trimming leaves on bushes.

'You know I'd never leave you behind, sure I would not, flower. That morning, I was only down – ' she lowered her voice so Miss MacFadyen would not hear – 'to the pawn man with the bangles from you-know-who. I had this notion to get us the ferry tickets for Dun Laoghaire. He always told me they were the finest gold in all the world.'

Jazz knew all about the box under the bed. Jazz sometimes used to pull it out and look at the things.

'But that skilly-eyed slyman in the pawn shop pockled me, would no give me more than a tenner for the lot. Can you beat it! I was that angry, I don't know, something came over me. I felt just that fashed with it all. I didn't mean on leaving you long. I didn't know they'd come and take you. Just something came over me.'

'It's no matter to me,' said Jazz, not looking Bridie in the eye. 'I'm away now to see my dad's place.' She had never called him her dad before. It sounded odd to her too.

'Och, flower, you're only trying to get across me, because you know I don't want you away over there.'

'That's grand then,' said Jazz. 'Because I'm going anyway. And I might never come back!' She wondered if Bridie knew about it being a return ticket and that she had to come back.

'*You've* set her up to this, sure you have!' Suddenly Bridie lost her temper and shouted at Miss MacFadyen. 'You're kidnapping her.'

'It's nothing to do with *them*,' said Jazz. 'Anyway, it's all fixed.'

Things kept moving so fast, almost too fast, and before she knew it, Jazz was being driven along the motorway to Prestwick Airport.

'Can't wait to get rid of me, can you?' Jazz said to Miss MacFadyen. She felt that the only creature in the foster household who was sad to see her leave was the goldfish.

'Why no, dear, that's not it at all. And if I were a wee mousie, I'd like to hide away in your case here, so I could get to see the world too.'

Jazz made a peelie-wally I'm-gonna-be-sick face.

26

3

A Sight of the World from on High

At the check-in desk Miss MacFadyen began to fuss with Jazz's luggage. 'Now, you're sure you'll be all right, dear, won't you?'

There was a cold lump like porridge lurking in Jazz's heart, or where she supposed her heart would be.

She did not want to go on this plane. She did not want to fly across the world. What if the world wasn't round after all, but flat like it looked in the atlas? She did not want to leave Scotland. She did not want to meet strangers. What would happen when she arrived? What would the people be like? Would she get a room of her own? Would she be allowed to watch telly? What stations did they get?

She wanted to go back to Bridie to say, 'Let's make it up.'

But it was too late for any of that.

'Course I'll be right fine,' she snarled. 'What d'you take me for? Some kind of stupid eejit?'

Jazz was more anxious than she had ever been in her life. The lump of cold fear was slipping down to somewhere just above her belly button. She felt sick with it.

'I'm telling you, I'm looking forward to getting away from all you lot,' she added, clenching her teeth. 'First time I've been on a plane.' First time I've been anywhere. Wish I was taking the ferry to Dun Laoghaire. Wish that lot had asked me to stay, not these other ones.

Miss MacFadyen smiled. 'You're a brave wee lass. And, look, your little outfit they want you to wear is just here. I packed it right at the top of your hand-luggage.'

'I know. I'm no a daftie.'

'Then you can reach it easily and slip it on in good time.

27

They'll want to recognise you at the other end.'

Miss MacFadyen picked up the case to hand it in to the clerk. Jazz snatched it back.

'I can do that,' she snapped. 'Been looking after myself for long enough, so I have.'

'Very well, dear.' Miss MacFadyen leaned forward and looked as though she wanted to kiss Jazz goodbye, or give her a hug. Jazz couldn't risk any scenes like that. It might make her want to hug Miss MacFadyen back and pretend she was hugging her mum. And then she'd cling on and then start to cry and then never let go and the whole thing would be over and she'd be back where she started.

And, if that happened, all the other passengers gathering at the check-in desk, in their strong blue turbans, and fluttering green saris and smart saffron-yellow veils, with their excited dark-eyed toddlers, and tired pale grandmas and huge bulging suitcases, and brand-new microwave ovens in boxes, would notice and stare.

Best to get it over with quick.

''Bye, Miss MacFadyen, and thanks for your help, and say "Hi" to Bridie for me,' said Jazz as lightly as though she had been travelling the globe, flat or round, all her life, and she turned away from Miss MacFadyen and into the control of the steely air steward who immediately hung a plastic wallet, marked UNACCOMPANIED MINOR, round Jazz's neck.

'What's that for?' Jazz said crossly. 'I'm no some piece of stray luggage. I do no need a label.'

But it seemed that, as a child travelling alone, she did.

'Your ticket and your passport's in there. Don't meddle with either,' said the air steward.

It also turned out that keeping close company with an air steward could be worse than spending any amount of time with a teacher or social worker.

'In fact, you know what, you're more like a prison warder than a human being, you are,' said Jazz. 'More than any other person I've ever met in my life. And I've met a few.'

'And so have I,' said the steward and her scarlet shiny smile did not even wobble as she led Jazz to her seat on the plane and buckled the safety belt.

'Right by the galley so I can keep an eye on you all the time,' said the steward with menace.

The rest of the passengers filed on afterwards, stowed their hand-baggage, found their seats. An elderly man in a red turban and a check suit took the place right next to Jazz. He pulled a rug round himself and immediately went to sleep. And still the plane didn't take off.

'Get on with it then,' Jazz said. 'Will we leave or will we not?'

The stewards read the safety regulations. It was worse than school. Then quite suddenly, with a lurch and a swoop, the plane took off, up and away.

The trip went on and on. Jazz got bored. She got up and wandered along the aisle to see what she could find. She found the first-class cabin. Here, the passengers, mostly men in suits, had bigger seats and looked as though they were having nicer food. Jazz found an empty seat and sat in it. The steward came looking for her.

'Go back to your own place and don't wander about, please,' she said.

Jazz said, 'Folks on buses change seats if they want.'

'This is not a bus.'

'Trains too.'

'Nor is it a train. Please return to your seat immediately.'

'Aye, prison warder, I'm on my way. Don't fash yourself.'

Jazz wanted to scuttle off and hide somewhere, as she usually did when an adult annoyed her. But flying through the air like an angel, all these millions of miles above the world, where was there to go to, apart from the cramped toilets down the far end of the aisle? And there was a queue of seven people waiting for those.

So Jazz slept for a while and woke as cross as ever. They still had not arrived. It already seemed a good deal longer than the ferry trip to Dun Laoghaire and that had lasted all day.

One of the other stewards brought Jazz a plastic envelope printed with pictures of teddies and balloons.

'It's our airline gift pack, dear. All the children travelling get one.'

Inside the pack were felt-tip pens, a red London double-decker bus, a storybook about a lost dog which they had in the reception class at St Mungo's, a pretend pilot's cap, and a colouring-in book with large simple pictures of decorated elephants in procession, palm trees and women picking the fresh green leaves from the tea bushes on a hillside.

Jazz took one quick look and handed it all back.

'How old d'you think I am? Colouring in? That's just for weans.'

Later, after the passengers had been served their dinners on plastic trays, another of the stewards came and asked Jazz if she'd like to visit the pilot's deck.

'And for what?'

'Not for anything. Just for interest. Most of the kids find it quite exciting to go and take a look, see how a plane is piloted.'

'Most of the kids, huh?'

'Specially the boys, but girls too.'

'Well, perhaps you can't tell the difference, but I'm not a boy, and I'm no "most of the kids". And I have no wish to see how your pilot does his job.'

Jazz found the adult travellers' gift pack which contained a miniature toothbrush, and a black sleeping mask.

'And perhaps you can no see that, right now, I'm trying to get some much-needed rest!' She pulled the mask down over her face to show she was sleeping.

Soon, the overhead lights in the cabin were turned down. The cabin was lit by an eerie half-light. A film was shown. You had to put on headphones to hear the soundtrack.

'Ancient history,' Jazz said, for Jennie Stewart had already seen it and told her the story. She was too tired to bother with it, now that Jennie had told her the ending.

Jazz slept. She dreamed scary dreams of being left alone in an empty place with rats. Just in time, before the rats got her, she heard Bridie say from a long way off, 'Angels guard you.' Then there was another dream of arriving in a strange palace built of sand where she was met by a decorated elephant.

She woke, then dozed again. She was aware of the steward sitting in a seat near by, kicking off her high-heeled shoes and snoring.

Suddenly Jazz woke to find the elderly man in the red turban and the rug prodding her in the ribs.

'Give over,' Jazz bellowed in her sleep. 'Will you no leave me alone?'

'Wake, young miss. Wake,' the old man said. 'Look! Please look out there! You must be looking now!'

He pointed through the oval window beside him.

'Behold! Yonder is the greatest wonder of our world.'

'Could've fooled me,' Jazz muttered. But she leaned across anyhow to see what was getting him in such a stushie.

At first, there seemed to be nothing but black darkness above, ahead and below. The plane with its three hundred sleeping people might have been floating through some terrible nightmare for all Jazz could see.

The old man made Jazz change places so she would be next to the window. 'The finest sight in the world,' he blethered on, turning his head slowly from side to side with emotion and wonder. 'Such a sight of the whole world as God must see it.'

God? What did this old fellow know about God?

Jazz peered again into the darkness outside and was a bit afraid at what she saw.

Beyond and below was not all just darkness and blackness. It was worse than that. Many miles beneath them was a miniature living land, coloured in white and brown and beige, but with no houses, no people, no trees, no living creatures of any kind, a terrifying and desolate world. It was spiked with rock points, and whiteness, and pink rocks, and dark shadowed valleys, and sheets of whiteness, everything being gradually lighted by a rosy pinkness of early morning.

'Our Himalayas,' said the old man, beaming as though he had created the desolate snowy mountains himself. 'The highest summits of the world, and the whole chain stretching for over a thousand miles.'

'So?' said Jazz. 'And *I've* been up Ben Nevis, the highest mountain in Scotland and all of Britain. And on my own two feet.'

This was not in fact true. Jazz had never been anywhere near Ben Nevis, nor even seen a photograph of it. It was a boy at school, who had left last year to go and live in Australia, who'd been taken to Ben Nevis as a farewell treat by his aunty. He'd told everybody about it.

'And Ben Nevis,' said Jazz, 'is four thousand feet high.'

The peaks over which they now travelled were, according to the old man, over six times higher than that.

But he didn't seem to be bragging, merely telling her.

Jazz wished she didn't have to tell lies. It never helped. But it was all Bridie's fault.

She told lies, so Jazz had to.

4

Garlanded with Golden Flowers

Jazz remembered arriving in Ireland, stepping off the ferry at Dun Laoghaire, to be mobbed by a crowd of cheerful chattering strangers, tall and short, tousled and tidy, all knowing her, yet she not knowing a single one of them.

Now, in a similar way, a colourful crowd drifted towards her across the arrivals lounge. They were like a flock of butterflies with their fluttering shawls and *dupatta* scarves and bright bobbing turbans.

Even though Jazz was wearing, not the rhubarb *salvar kameez*, but her Kool Kats sweatshirt, her jeans and her Lone Star Rider trainers, they recognised which one she was.

Hands together in greeting, they swept up to her. 'Sat sri akal,' they said, one after another, whatever that meant.

Jazz gaped. Each of the adult relatives took turns to bow to her, to touch the crown of her head. She wondered which one was Rajinder's mother and which was his father, if he had had a father. Bridie never spoke of either.

How could she ask? The grown-ups were all chattering away to each other in Punjabi.

Jazz was garlanded with golden flowers around her neck, and smiled at. She wondered, perhaps she really was some important sort of a princess, just like her friend Jennie used to tell her. Jennie Stewart had been to France so she knew tons of things about the world, or thought she did.

'You never know, Jazz, you might be someone ever so royal, especially if your dad was. India's full of that kind of stuff, palaces and princes.'

However, when Jazz had mentioned palaces and princes to

Miss MacFadyen, Miss MacFadyen had merely said, 'No, my dear, I rather think not. I believe you'll find they're hard-working farming folk, country people. Though I'm sure you'll have a lovely time if you put your mind to it, even if it *is* a bit different from what you're used to.'

Arriving in Ireland that time, she'd had Bridie there to protect her, to explain her to the rellies. Now she just stood and grinned. What else was she supposed to do with them all bowing down to her?

The boys each made a respectful bow to Jazz, then quickly turned away, more interested in aircraft landing on the runways outside. But the older girls crowded round. They wanted to touch her hair, to hold her arm, to take turns to be allowed to walk next to her and chatter to her even though she didn't understand. Jazz had never been popular like this before. It felt odd.

'I am your cousin Harjit,' said the tallest of them. 'And this is Surinder, and Kuldeep, and Pritpal.'

Jazz wondered if she was going to be able to remember their names and tell them apart. Harjit was in the red *dupatta* scarf, Surinder in the green, Kuldeep in brown, Pritpal in ochre.

It didn't seem to bother the grown-ups that they couldn't speak English. They made do with smiles and gestures, with shouting cheerfully at Jazz in Punjabi and with chattering about her. She could tell they were talking about her. They kept pointing. It was her clothes they looked at most.

'You never seen Lone Star trainers before?' Jazz muttered.

They all trooped out to a strange minibus with wooden sides, painted all over with multi-coloured patterns like something from a fairground, and hung outside and in with tinsel and flags and paper flowers. The windscreen was decorated with coloured prayer cards and coloured fairy lights blinking on and off in front of the driver's face. It seemed that it didn't belong to any of them but that they'd borrowed it specially to come to the Mahatma Gandhi Airport to fetch Jazz.

Jazz was put to sit in the front. It was meant to be a place of honour. She was squeezed between two large sweaty aunts, and a younger uncle, or perhaps he was an older cousin, who was driving. The rest of them had to pack in on the hard benches behind. In the front you could see out. At the back, you couldn't see anything much.

'Delhi!' one of the aunts yelled in Jazz's ear. 'Delhi, Delhi!'

One of the cousins in the back translated. 'Aunty is saying how we will now be showing you fine city of New Delhi. Great sights. Taj Mahal. Red Fort. OK? Everything! Wonderful time!'

It was a big day out for them. They were making the most of having the bus. Once, when Mrs Macpherson had been explaining to the class how Sikhs, along with many other faiths in the world, did not have Christmas, Jazz had felt quite sorry for them. Now she could see they had worked out other ways of having fun. And she felt sorry for herself instead. She longed to be allowed to sleep.

Jazz used to think St Enoch's shopping centre on a Saturday was busy when everybody seemed to be on the move at once. Here, pressing up around them were trucks, and bicycles, and beggars, and handcarts, stray dogs and pedestrians who, if they'd any sense, ought to have known about keeping to the pavements, if only there had been any. There was so much noise of auto-rickshaws revving, scooters beeping, taxis roaring, and policemen shouting as they tried to untangle the flow. It was more muddled than the school playground at going-home time.

The side of the roads were just as chaotic. Jazz saw at least a thousand hundred million people getting on with their lives right out in the open, with not a crack of space where somebody wasn't sitting, or sleeping, eating, talking, selling something, begging, wandering, pushing something along, or leading goats through it.

And everywhere, Jazz saw cows, with black noses and big sad eyes. They wandered slowly amongst the people. They

35

lay down to rest. They stood quite still thinking, right in the middle of the traffic. Jazz wondered how they got used to the noise.

'In our village,' whispered one of the girl cousins over Jazz's shoulder, 'the cows do not do this. We do not allow them to wander freely or they would trample the crops.' It was the one with the red *dupatta* over her shoulders, called Harjit. 'And in our village, it is peaceful. Not noisy like this.'

'Grand,' said Jazz. 'Because that's what I'm used to.'

One of the baby cousins in the back of the van began crying.

'And I specially can no bide the sound of a deaving wean.'

The day's outing dragged on with so many important sights that had to be seen. Jazz saw the crowds and the cows and the hot sky, but noticed few of the sights. The garland of marigolds round her neck wilted. She woke with a jolt as the van swerved round a man in a white cap leading two dappled goats down the road.

'Now we stop for refreshment.' One of the cousins touched Jazz's arm to tell her. 'You will enjoy our Indian tea. It is excellent and refreshing.'

The minibus had pulled off the road in an empty landscape, nothing but scrub and bushes. Everybody piled out.

Immediately, the empty landscape filled with people rushing towards them trying to sell them things and to stare at Jazz. The uncles shooed them away.

'They have not seen an English girl before. So they are inquisitive,' said the cousin in red.

'I'm no English, never have been. I'm Glaswegian, Scottish.'

Under a bare thorn tree was a wooden stall. The tea-man began brewing up a fistful of black leaves out of a box, some condensed milk out of a tin, loads of sugar, and a handful of what looked to Jazz like dried peas, over a little fire in a tin can on his table.

'Right fykie way to try and make tea,' said Jazz, but nobody heard because the boys were swinging on the tree, the girls were minding the toddlers, the aunts were gossiping and fanning themselves and all the uncles were admiring the oily engine of the minibus.

Jazz was handed a tea glass so hot she nearly dropped it.

She took a sip.

'Eeergh,' she said and spat it out. It was like the black boiled-up treacle in the Jedburgh candy that the old widow in the flat downstairs used to make. Bridie said it was bad for you to eat sweet things. If Jazz took more than half a teaspoonful of sugar, Bridie used to say, 'You like it that sickly because you're one of them little darkie Indians, aren't you?'

Then Jazz would yell at her.

'This kind of tea's disgusting,' said Jazz. 'All spicy and syrupy.'

One of the aunts took it away with a smile and a sideways shake of her head. One of the uncles bought from the tea-man something in a bottle called *Gold Spot* which sounded hopeful. It was as bright as paint water. Jazz wondered if it was poison. But it tasted all right, sweet, fizzy and warm.

Everyone else drank the thick tea smiling, then piled back into the vehicle.

Hours later, they arrived to find a whole load more people, all the old ones who'd stayed behind, waiting for them. The respectful greetings began all over again.

'That's weird, the whole lot of you all living in the same house,' said Jazz, except it wasn't so much of a house, as an open courtyard with a few tiny rooms opening off it.

There was a patient group of neighbours and neighbours' children waiting outside the courtyard to get a glimpse of Jazz's arrival. There was also a miserable dog with bald patches in its fur.

Jazz could tell they must be country folk, just like Miss MacFadyen had said. They were not covered with jewel pins and diamond nose-rings like some of the people she'd seen in

New Delhi. Nor were the men's turbans crisply pleated and held with gold-headed pins like the smart Sikh businessmen in silk suits on the plane, but were wrapped loosely round their heads. Nor were their beards neatly combed and rolled into tight chin-straps but were long and straggling.

'I want to go to bed,' said Jazz. 'Now.' She wanted to get away.

'First you must eat. There is a chicken, especially for you. The best we have. With knife and fork for you.'

Jazz wondered what was so special about a knife and fork. The cousin told her how they'd been specially borrowed from the teacher next door.

It was mostly the one in red who did the talking. She seemed to be the oldest of the girl cousins and she also spoke the best English. She'd been to Europe for three months, so she said, to stay with other relatives in Southall.

'Just like you have come here to stay with us. Sikh people are great travellers.'

'Are they?' said Jazz.

'Indeed, yes. If you look about, you will see that the world is so full of Punjabi people travelling. Yet they always leave their hearts here in the land of the five rivers.'

Jazz decided she didn't care for the cousin in red. She knew too much.

To show that she too was well travelled, Jazz pretended to know where Southall was.

'Aye, Southall, that's a grand place. Near enough to Glasgow, though I've not yet been there myself.'

'Southall is in the county of Middlesex, quite near to London where the buses are red,' said Harjit.

Jazz disliked her even more. 'We have red buses in Glasgow too,' she said angrily. 'And green ones, and yellow.'

Jazz's chicken supper was served to her in one of the small rooms off the courtyard. Because she was so important, a chair was fetched for her from the teacher's house. She sat alone at the table.

Jazz said, 'I don't eat Indian food. All that spice, it's that hot. It burns your lips.'

'Ah no, Cousin,' said Harjit. 'It will be all right for you. Our food is never hot and burning in that way. And as well, Aunty has lessened the peppers for you so you need not be frightened to eat.'

As a succession of white china dishes were set before her, the smaller children gathered in the open doorway to watch.

'What about your supper? Will you wee folks no be getting your tea too?' Jazz asked. 'Och well, suit yourselves.'

Jazz had a brief moment of wishing she'd kept the gift pack from the airline so she'd have had something to offer them as a present. But she put the skellie thought quickly from her mind. After all, *she* was the visitor, so they had to give *her* things.

Jazz didn't recognise much of the food, only the chicken, the vegetables and the sloppy dahl.

The aunts and the cousins kept on bringing her more.

Jazz said, 'I'm fou as a puggie. And you know what we say about Indian carry-outs back home? We say they're a right rip-off. They fill you up so you're that full. Then half an hour on, you're half starving again. That's the fault with Indian food. It's so much rice.'

The cousin who knew about the buses in Middlesex didn't know what a rip-off was for she just smiled.

'I regret, Cousin, that we are not eating so much rice here,' she said. 'Only for weddings and feasts. Other days, we eat chapattis and vegetables.'

She pointed to the pile of flat bread, round as pancakes, keeping warm in a basket. There was also a tin beaker of something white and lumpy which looked like sick but smelled like yoghurt.

'For you to drink. It is curds from the milk of our buffalo,' explained the cousin.

Even thinking about buffalo's milk, let alone drinking it, made Jazz think she'd be sick.

Nobody else ate a morsel until Jazz had finished. Then they ate theirs, not in the cramped room with Jazz, but outside in the courtyard, sitting on the ground, each person's food in three tin bowls on a tin tray. There were so many people in the household that it took ages to serve them all.

At last it was time for bed. Jazz was shown to a hard platform with a cotton quilt on it in another of the small rooms off the courtyard. There was a tiny window, with bars across.

Jazz didn't realise that the other four girls were going to sleep in here too. They all piled in and, by candlelight, unrolled their bed-rolls on the cold floor and lay down.

'All you lot sleeping in here too?' said Jazz, irritated.

'Always the guest has the bed,' replied one of them, but in the dark Jazz couldn't tell which.

'Well, if you start chattering, I'll never get any sleep.'

'Surely you would not wish to sleep quite by yourself, alone?' said one of them. 'That would be upon all our heads for treating you unkindly.'

Lying on the hard bed Jazz, who had been longing all day to sleep, was now wide awake. In the cramped room, filled with the gentle sound of new cousins breathing, she was desolate and lonely.

She wanted to cry herself to sleep. But with the other girls on their bed-rolls on the floor, how could she dare? It would wake them. They would hear. And then they would laugh.

Jazz wondered what Bridie was doing. The clocks were different in Scotland. Perhaps it wasn't even night-time there. If Bridie were around now, she'd creep over and whisper in Jazz's ear. After that, Jazz would be able to sleep.

But Bridie wasn't here. Jazz had to whisper it to herself.

'God bless and sleep tight. Angels guard you till it's light.'

It wasn't quite the same.

Jazz thought, why am I here and how did I get here?

She wasn't sure if she could remember and she had an uneasy feeling that things weren't going to go the way she wanted.

5

The Sound of God

At the deepest part of night, Jazz was terrified out of sleep by an unearthly noise. A ghostly old man's voice quavered through the darkness like the sound of God.

Jazz sat upright. 'Och fegs!' she gasped. 'What's going on?'

The angels you prayed to, when you remembered, were supposed to prevent this kind of thing happening.

The voice, which seemed to be right there in the room, yet far away at the same time, boomed on, in the language Jazz could not understand, with crackles and rustles of pages turning.

The sleepy voice of the one of the girl cousins tried to be reassuring.

'Ssh. It is all no worry. We have a loudspeaker on the tower of the temple. The holy man of our village reads to us every morning.'

'Morning? Middle of the night, more like! Some folks are still trying to sleep,' said Jazz.

'It is good to hear the scriptures of the holy book. With the loudspeaker all may benefit without stirring even from their homes.'

'And what if they don't happen to want to listen?'

'He tells us how God's bounty belongs to all.'

'Could he no wait to tell us all about it in the morning?' Jazz grumbled as she tried to get back to sleep.

When the holy man's chanting was finally silent, the morning began with a new set of noises. Churns clanged. Water buckets splashed at the pump. Uncles coughed.

Animal hooves clattered and the little ones chattered or wailed. It wasn't even light yet but it was already time to be up.

The cousins did not wear the same colours as the day before, which was irritating of them. Jazz had to sort out all over again who was who.

Harjit, today wearing a paintbox-green *dupatta* with an amber-coloured *salvar kameez*, asked Jazz, 'Cousin, why do you wear these same garments as the day before? Do you not also wish to change?' Harjit was the one who liked telling Jazz things even if Jazz didn't want to know.

'No,' said Jazz firmly. 'This is my best favourite sweatshirt and I'm probably going to wear it every single moment I have to be here.'

'Is it not better to be refreshed each day with other garments?' said Harjit. 'If you have no garments, I will lend some.'

'Not likely,' said Jazz. 'No one's getting me dressed up like I'm a foreigner.' She had already pushed the pink *salvar kameez* to the bottom of her case so that everybody could forget it existed.

Jazz also resisted the cousins' encouragements to wash from a bucket of chill water drawn fresh from the pump.

'All this washing, it's that unhealthy. Rajinder went in for the same thing, my mother said, and look what it did to him! Washed himself clean away.'

'But, Cousin, is it not refreshing to feel oneself clean each morning?' Harjit said.

'Och no. A body needs to keep on a wee bit of dirt to warm it. Did no one bother to tell you?'

Later, Harjit offered to lend Jazz a pair of her own sandals .to wear instead of trainers.

You were supposed to take off your shoes and leave them by the doorway before you entered a room. It was quick enough for the other girls to slip out of their sandals. But it took Jazz ages each time, untying the long laces of Lone Star

42

trainers. So she didn't bother. She just kept them on.

Nobody said anything. But Jazz could tell that they noticed and didn't approve, specially when Harjit came running back with a pair of sandals which she tried to make Jazz borrow. They were made of green plastic. 'Look, see, Cousin. For you to wear. If you like them, you may keep them.'

'Yukky-do!' said Jazz. 'Green plastic, yerk!' She refused to take them. 'Green may be fine and dandy for cabbages. But not for me, ta very much.'

The girls clustered round her like a flight of fancy-coloured birds, giggling, chatting, smiling, offering to lend her things, trying to be nice to her.

'Give over,' said Jazz. 'You're stifling me.' Jazz went into the dark hut at the side of the courtyard, with the deep black hole in the ground which was the toilet, just to get away from them.

They waited for her outside.

'Everything OK in there, Sis?' one of them whispered through the slats of the door.

Jazz tried not answering.

'Sis, you need me to fetch you more water?'

They called each other Sister or Sis, even when they weren't. So now they were daring to call Jazz their Sis too.

'I'm *not* your sister,' Jazz shouted back through the door. She had always wanted a sister, a real sister, a big one, a baby one, one to fight with, any kind of sister would do. When she complained to Bridie, Bridie had said it was hardly her fault Jazz had no sister. She meant that it was Rajinder's fault for letting himself die.

'You sure you are all right in there?' Harjit and Kuldeep barged right in.

'You're so nosy,' said Jazz. 'Can I no go even in the jacks without being followed?'

'Please, we are not wishing to be inquisitive. But dishonour will come to us if we are not taking good care of

43

you. And we feared you had fallen down the hole deep into the ground.'

So much for Miss MacFadyen saying she'd have a lovely time! What did a social worker know about anything? Jazz was having a horrible time. And being an important guest didn't last long either.

By mid-morning the borrowed chair had been carried back to the neighbour's house. So had the fork, knife, spoon and the white china. Jazz was just another girl. Girls were served nearly last, after the adult men of the family, after the teenage boys of the family, after the two hired workers, after the younger aunts, after the youngest aunt who seemed to Jazz to be especially fat and lazy, for she hardly ever bothered to get up and do anything to help.

When Jazz asked what her name was, Harjit quickly said that it was Aunty.

They were all called Aunty, or Auntiji, just as all the uncles were Uncleji. It made it difficult to work out which aunts and uncles belonged together, which toddler belonged to which aunty, or which of the older ones were whose grandparents.

'It is respectful,' Harjit explained. 'To say it this way. It is not so respectful for us to say the name. We show respect to all who are older and more senior.'

Forcing down her beakerful of buffalo curds while squatting on the ground with her back against the wall, Jazz knew it was going to be worse than even Bridie had said.

Jennie Stewart had been wrong when she'd told Jazz that she was some sort of Indian princess.

Miss MacFadyen had, as usual, been sort of right.

Rajinder's people were not only country culchies. They were poor. They didn't even have any chairs of their own but squatted on their heels. They ate with their fingers. The little children didn't have toys or books. When they played, they made do with each other or with the half-bald dog.

For so long, Jazz had been longing for slippers that looked

44

like a pair of fluffy-faced puppies. And here she ended up with a bald dog for company. It just wasn't fair.

The only things these people had were a couple of fields and a lot of hard work. The girls were given an enormous heap of chickpeas to be sorted through. They had to pick out the bits of dirt and grit. They had just begun when one of the uncles came across the courtyard towards them carefully carrying a bottle of ink, a pen and a flimsy sheet of pale blue airmail paper. The chair from next door was borrowed again, also a wicker table.

Jazz wondered if he was the one who was Rajinder's father. She hoped he wasn't. He looked so very old. Jazz thought he must be the oldest person she'd ever seen, though he still went out to the fields. His turban was white. So was his beard, long and bushy like the Santa Claus that Bridie had taken Jazz to see in Foster Brothers on Argyll Street last year.

As he came over to Jazz and greeted her with his hands together, without even thinking about it, Jazz found herself jumping upright, placing her own hands together and bowing her head in reply to the old man before taking the paper he held out to her.

She started to ask him, 'Did you know Rajinder?' But Harjit interrupted her.

'Uncleji is very deaf. He no longer hears. And he does not speak English.'

'You translate for me then. Ask him about Rajinder for me.'

'I do not think that Uncleji likes to hear that name spoken. It distresses him.'

The old man began to speak to Jazz, very slowly, in Punjabi. Even though Jazz didn't understand a word of what he said, she somehow got the meaning. He was telling her she must write a letter. And it was obvious, somehow, who he wanted her to write to.

'Sure,' said Jazz. 'Anything to get out of sorting silly old chickpeas.'

45

Harjit said, 'Uncleji is asking if you will write to your mother.'

'I know, I know,' said Jazz impatiently. 'I'm no a daftie.'

She sat at the little table. The pen was the old-fashioned kind with a wooden holder and a steel nib like the ones they let you have a go with in the Scotland Street School Museum. They went there once on a class outing. You had to keep dipping the nib into the inkpot and then it made splodges as you wrote. Jazz felt shy with everybody watching her. She was never very good at writing, even with a proper Biro. She didn't want anybody to read what she was writing.

She wrote:

> *Dear Bridie,*
>
> *I have arived I had a fantastick pure dead magic trip here. They met me in a majical goldin coach. It is a sort of palase here.*
>
> *I have six servants of my own who look after me We eat feests of peacock every day and many other lovly thigs. Mornings, I go riding on a decarated elephant on the back green Love and all the best from Jazz.*

The old man watched, nodding his head, as Jazz wrote the address on the envelope. Jazz wondered if he could read English even if he couldn't speak it.

When Jazz had stuck up the envelope, the old man called one of the aunts, who pulled her *dupatta* up over her head, then beckoned for Jazz to follow, out of the courtyard, down the narrow alleyways between the houses. Four cousins came too, and Fat Lazy Aunty, waddling slowly like a duck.

The postbox was a rusty tin cylinder with a lid, dangling from a hook on a wall on the side of someone's house. There were no words or numbers on the tin. It didn't look as though the mail got collected very often. Jazz wondered if the letter would ever reach Scotland. If it did, she knew it would really annoy Bridie to hear about all the servants looking after her, because if Jazz wouldn't run an errand or help with the dishes, Bridie used to yell at her, 'You're so idle you need a servant to take care of you, my girl, and that's the truth.'

Jazz hoped that if the letter did reach Bridie, she'd start missing her a lot, perhaps even so much that she'd write back.

As Jazz shoved the blue envelope down into the rusty box, everybody smiled their approval. But Jazz realised she'd written all the wrong things. She shouldn't have said all that about servants and feasts which anyway weren't even a quarter true. She should have written,

> Dear Bridie,
>   Please come and get me quick, I canna bide it here. Please come to get me at once.

But it was too late. She couldn't change what she'd written now. Besides, she couldn't really have Bridie fetching her away, for Miss MacFadyen would be bound to make her go back to stay with the goldfish couple. That would be almost as bad as sorting chickpeas.

Everybody sauntered back along the alleys but Jazz ran ahead, and as soon as she reached the courtyard, she dived into the dark toilet hut, crouched on the floor with her back against the door so nobody could get in, not even those guardian angels who Bridie had promised would be looking after her so long as she said her prayers, and she growled very quietly to herself while she tried to think what to do to really annoy these people.

6

Fields of Paradise

She had to come out, eventually. Someone else needed to use the toilet.

Harjit tried to be friendly. 'Come with us, Cousin,' she said. 'We wish to show you the most beautiful view in all of the Punjab.'

The girls led Jazz up onto the roof of the house. They wanted to show her the family fields. Harjit spoke of them as though they were some kind of paradise.

There was no proper staircase, just a steep flight of crumbling brick steps up an outside wall. From the flat mud rooftop, you could see the farm lands stretching towards the trees by the canal. Near by, the countryside looked green. It faded to dusty blue in the distance. Overhead was a flight of green parrots, as bright as Harjit's vivid sandals. They whizzed through the air, then dived for the trees squarking like quarrelsome schoolchildren.

The dark dots amongs the faraway crops were the men at work. The big dots were the buffaloes and the wooden carts.

Were those men Rajinder's brothers? Or were they the husbands of his sisters? Had Rajinder worked in those fields when he was young, just like the dark dots? Jazz wanted to know things. But she didn't know the right way to ask, that would make Harjit give a straight answer.

Jazz asked, 'Which ones are Rajinder's brothers?'

Harjit replied, 'We are all one family. And up here on the rooftop, we place the hot chillies to dry in the sun.' She pointed out the red pods, spread on a white sheet. 'And also from up here, the boys may fly their kites.'

A dozen coloured paper squares were dancing and jostling in the sky, higher even than where the parrots flew, being flown from other rooftops in the village.

Jazz wanted to know if Rajinder had flown a kite from this same rooftop when he'd been her age and, if so, what colour it might have been. There was a tangle of flimsy green tissue paper and pink plastic string lying on the dried mud floor. Jazz picked it up and flung it upwards. But it wouldn't catch the air, just kept tumbling down.

'It's that fykie to get it launched!' she said. 'What's the knack to do it right? Do you have your own kite? Shall we fly it now? Will you show me how?'

Harjit replied, 'Only boys may fly kites. It is their recreation. Girls do not fly kites. We have better things to do with our time.'

Jazz agreed. 'Kite flying!' she said with a shrug. 'Big deal.'

From the rooftop, you could peer over the parapet wall and down onto the courtyard below and see the family working. Viewed from so high, the aunties, in their fluttering coloured shawls, appeared not to be walking across the yard but floating this way and that, like petals on water.

Jazz wondered which of them were his sisters, which had known him when he was young. But again she must have asked it wrong, for Harjit replied, 'A bride always takes her husband's sisters as her own.'

Jazz tried again. This time she asked about the bride chosen before Rajinder met up with Bridie in the ladies' bar of *The Rubaiyat*. 'You know, the person he was *supposed* to marry. What happened to her?'

Harjit lowered her eyes.

'The family was dishonoured.'

'Which family?'

Harjit, still looking at the ground, said, 'And the dowry was returned. That is the custom. If the marriage does not take place.'

'The dowry?'

'Please, Sister, you do not ask. It is not respectful.'

It was pointless talking to Harjit. She didn't even try to understand what Jazz was on about.

So what was it that Jazz wanted to hear? Now she wasn't sure if she knew what the right questions were, let alone the right answers.

She said, 'Well, it's a right carfuffle, the way you all live muddled together. It's a wee wonder you can tell your own mothers apart.'

Kulpal and Surinder giggled, covering their faces with their *dupattas*.

Harjit said, 'We know our mothers. Sukvinder Kaur, that is my mother's name. But it is not respectful to say this. It is respectful to call her Aunty. Or you may call her Auntiji for greater respect. Here, all are one family. All here are your family.'

They were too eager to accept her, without even asking whether she wanted it. It was a waste of their effort.

'Who said I even wanted to be in this family?' Jazz said. Looking down into the courtyard, she thought how much she hated them all. She picked a flake of dried yellow mud off the roof and flicked it over the edge. It floated gently to land on one of the aunties' heads. She brushed it away with her hand. She didn't seem to realise where it had come from.

Being high up on the rooftop was a bit like being God. You could see them, they couldn't see you. Jazz remembered Bridie once telling her how God sat up high in order to be able to watch everything and everybody at the same time. If you were God, you'd be able to make things happen to the world below, like storms and earthquakes.

It would be interesting, Jazz thought, to throw something a bit heavier than a flake of mud. A huge ice block would do fine. It would smash into little bits when it landed. But there were no ice blocks handy.

Or just a piece of rock, like a boulder off the side of Glencoe. Or a bathtub full of soapy water.

Over in Galway, they didn't have the plumbing and they took a bath in a tin tub pulled into the front room. When the boys took it out to empty, it made a huge big splursh into the stream.

Or what if she threw herself? That would shake them up a bit.

Jazz thought about it for half a micro-second. She reckoned she knew how long half a micro-second was because Mrs Macpherson had once told them about time being relative. So time could be long or short, depending what you were doing at the time. Here it seemed to be long.

Jazz decided not to throw herself. The courtyard was too far down, and hard. Landing would hurt.

'Have you ever thought,' she said aloud to the cousins, 'that if someone dropped something from up here onto one of the aunties' heads, and then crouched low and hid, they'd never know where it had come from? So what if we brought a can of water up? Then we could tip it over!'

Harjit said, 'This would be foolish and of no use.'

'No,' said Jazz. 'It would be funny. They'd think it was suddenly raining.'

She looked round for something else interesting to drop into the courtyard. She saw the chilli pods drying on the sheet. She scooped up handfuls and before any of them could stop her, she flung them over the edge. They fell through the air like big scarlet wings. Some landed on a basket of damp washing. One landed on the dog's back, several in the food that was being prepared, and others fell right into the fire where they burned up with a quick flame.

One of the aunties glanced up looking startled, then irritated. She made clucking sounds of disapproval with her tongue but she did not stop her work.

Jazz sniggered. 'How's that for hot flying chillies?' she said.

But the others were hurrying down the broken brick steps looking alarmed.

Only Harjit waited for Jazz. She said, 'Cousin, you should not do foolish actions. We will all be chastised. And also it is not respectful.'

'What's all this respect about? You go bowing and scraping to the old folks every time you look at them. It's no natural to be bending down and touching their feet like that.'

'It is our custom,' said Harjit.

'Och fegs, you're all so straight. Can you no loosen up? It's no wonder you're all so dour if you never let yourselves enjoy a joke. Maybe that's why Rajinder had to get away, just to find a decent laugh? Because there's certainly no laughs round here.'

How could anyone be happy here, when all the day through there were so many jobs to be done? When the girls weren't having to pick over the huge mounds of dried lentils, they had to sort fresh coriander leaves, taking out the mouldy bits. Then they had to fetch in fuel, and after that help grind spices in a stone bowl.

'This the Stone Age, or what?' Jazz grumbled. 'It's all just jobs, jobs, jobs. Why have I to do all this? I'm supposed to be your guest.'

The job of making the cow-dung patties for burning on the cooking fire was, in fact, turning out to be quite fun. It reminded Jazz of being back at day nursery, in the Play Doh corner. The girls showed her how you had to pick up a handful of brown dung with your bare hands, mix it with dry straw, shape it, then fling it against an outside wall to dry in the sun.

They didn't see any harm in any of the work.

'We are all one family here,' said Harjit. 'So we all work together. Punjab is a good place. We are fortunate here in many ways. For one thing, we have a good water supply.'

'Big deal!' said Jazz.

'Indeed it is lucky. For in many areas the people do not yet have their own supply. They must go to the public pump every day. Now that really is hard work! And our cousin

52

would not be strong enough for it. Not till she had stayed with us for at least a year and eaten enough *mackay roti* with mustard spinach to make her big!'

'Yes I would. I'm very strong.' Jazz remembered how she'd wrestled Angus McLeod to the ground outside the cloakrooms one breaktime when he'd dared call her a Paki.

'Go on then, prove you aren't!' he'd jeered. But Jazz couldn't prove it because she hadn't really known what it meant. She just knew it was an insult. So she hit him.

Remembering that fight made Jazz cross.

'I've had it up to here with dung patties,' she said. 'I didn't come all this way to play with cow poo. It's against my civil liberties.' She dropped a half-made fuel patty on the ground and walked away fast, though she had no idea where to go.

One of the girls put down her own patty, and joined Jazz as she walked, slipping her arm casually through Jazz's, chatting politely with her as they went. It was cousin Pritpal who spoke only Punjabi, though dotted with English words like 'lipstick', 'disco' and 'have a nice time'. The only thing to stop the chatty creature blethering on was for both of them to turn round and head back to the dung pile.

The boys had jobs too. Theirs looked to Jazz much more interesting. 'So how come *they* get all the decent jobs?'

The boys went out to cut grass from beside their fields and dragged it home in a hessian sack. They led the goat out to graze at the end of a long stout rope which the goat kept trying to bite through. They took the buffaloes down to the canal. They worked the big machine with a huge steel blade which chopped livestock fodder into tiny pieces.

Back at St Mungo's Road Primary, Jazz was always getting into trouble, usually with the boys, usually for taunting them, then fighting them.

'Why do you fight so much?' Mrs Macpherson had asked her once.

'Because all boys deserve to be dead.'

'Funny idea,' Mrs Macpherson had said.

53

Here, there seemed less time for fighting. The boys and the uncles got on with their work while the aunts and girls got on with theirs. Everybody had to work, even the bald dog. Its job was to watch out for rats trying to get into the grainstore.

All the work was to do with food. Either it was about feeding the animals, or else about feeding the family. They were busy every moment of the day, yet time dragged along so slowly that each boring minute lasted for hours.

Jazz said to Harjit, 'You're all poor here, aren't you? And you know what, you must be dead stupid if you don't mind being poor.'

Harjit looked confused. 'We are not poor. Why should we be?'

'Yes you are. I've seen it on telly. Everyone in India's poor and starving.'

'Punjab, that means land of the five rivers. The rivers bring water to make the land flourish. Everyone works, and the farmers prosper.'

'You mean, everyone's yukky and horrible and poor.' Even as she said it, Jazz realised that she had not actually seen anybody in the village who looked as though they were starving, or begging or sleeping on a stairway, or even hungry and miserable like they sometimes did hanging round in Paddy's Market.

It was also true, though she didn't want to say it, that she herself hadn't once felt hungry since she arrived. In fact, quite often, she'd felt too full. Although it was always the same food twice a day – curds, spiced vegetables, dahl and chapattis – there was enough of it.

'Food, food, food, that's all you lot ever think about. How can you do that when Indians are supposed to be starving? I'm telling you, I canna bide this place. I want out. If those aunts make us do one more mucky job I'll run away.'

'Oh no, please do not do this,' said Harjit. 'It would cause much upset. And harm might come to you for you would not know where to go.'

'Ha Ha! that's what *you* think,' said Jazz, trying to look mysterious.

Jazz ran away from St Mungo's some days, especially if she was bored. She always let someone know when she was going to do it. And she never ran further than the shops at the end of St Mungo's Road so that they'd find her easily. Running away and then being found was good. She got taken back to sit in the secretary's office. At breaktime, Mrs Macpherson would come along to fetch her and give her a talking-to, and a quick hug too if none of the other staff was watching.

Jazz decided she must either run away or else pick a fight with someone. She didn't mind who. She dared herself to have a go at the fat aunt who was lying about doing nothing.

Although the family had no chairs, they had a day-bed which they called a *charpoi*, made of wood and string. Every morning, someone carried this *charpoi* out to the courtyard for Fat Aunt to lie on, with cushions under her head and people bringing her glasses of hot spicy tea. Jazz could see she wasn't just fat and lazy. She was spoiled senseless with it. The only time she bothered to get up was to go and change her *salvar kameez* for an even more decorated one, or to put on even prettier sandals.

So Jazz kicked the leg of the *charpoi*, at first almost accidentally, then a few more times.

Fat Aunt looked up. She said something that sounded almost friendly. Jazz wished she'd told her off then she could have pouted and answered back. That would have started a good row.

So Jazz tried picking a fight with one of the toddlers instead. He laughed and clapped his chubby hands together. Jazz tried to get into a fight with the bald dog by making a grab at the crust of leftover chapatti it was eating. The dog cringed and ran away, leaving the half-eaten chapatti behind.

The girls were sorting a basketful of beans. Jazz stood behind Kuldeep and pointed out each bit of grit she missed.

Kuldeep said, 'Not to bother with this work, Sis, if you are tired.'

Jazz sat by the day's pile of fuel to wait for someone to annoy her. Then she would leap up and argue with them.

As she sat there she saw that, cross though she was, there was another person on the far side of the couryard who was even crosser.

7

Granny Laugh, Granny Cry

It was the oldest of the aunts. They called her Oldest Auntiji. She was crouched beside the cooking fire preparing chapattis. Jazz scowled at her. Oldest Auntiji glared back, then muttered something into the fire. She was the grandmother. So she was Jazz's grandmother too.

Jennie Stewart had a grandmother. She called her 'Nan'.

Jennie's Nan wore a neat woollen skirt. She had curly permed hair and blue on her eyelids. She kept treacle twists in her handbag to offer to the children in the playground.

That was the kind of grandmother Jazz wanted, not this poor, worn-out old creature with cracked nails and rough skin.

Jennie's Nan fetched Jennie from school and took her downtown to St Enoch's Centre. Jennie's Nan bought her nice things, dancing shoes and sparkly tights, even when it wasn't her birthday. After shopping, Jennie's Nan took her out for tea at Mackie's Tea Rooms.

Oldest Auntiji never went anywhere. Jazz never saw her leave the courtyard to go out and admire the fields or into the village to gossip as the other aunts did.

Occasionally, she flung an order to one of the aunts or the girls if they looked as though they weren't doing anything useful, but never to the boys. When the boys had done their work, they were free to go out into the alley to play cricket or up onto the flat rooftop to fly their kites.

Once Jazz had wanted a grandmother even more than she had wanted a baby sister. But why did it have to be this one?

Jazz asked Harjit, 'What's she blethering on about?'

'She is telling her usual story, how life was better in past times. Everything was perfection until she was obliged to quit her own village when the Punjab was divided by the government. She is forgetting to say also that four of her children died. I would not wish for *my* babies to die. *I* believe our lives are better now than before. Women have babies and the babies live.'

Jazz watched Oldest Auntiji kneading and stretching the dough for the chapattis and she thought of Bridie trying to cook. Bridie didn't know how to bake anything except lumpy soda bread. It wasn't very nice. But if that's all there was, then you ate it.

Jazz wanted to be able to tell someone about Bridie's way of making a not-very-nice soda loaf, because telling about it might make it seem not so far away. But she didn't know who to tell it to, not so they would understand.

Oldest Auntiji held out to Jazz some colourful titbits like small cakes.

Harjit said, 'She is offering you sweetmeats. *Barfi* and *laddu*. The white ones are with coconut, the yellow ones with almonds, the green ones with pistachio nuts.'

Jazz said, 'How can I make friends with her when we don't even *understand* each other? That's just stupid.'

Like the sweet tea which was thick and creamy as a milkshake, the Indian sweets were too sickly. Jazz didn't like them.

'Tell her I'm no her pet dog,' she snarled. 'And I dinna take bribes.'

When Jazz refused the bright yellow *barfi* ball, Oldest Auntiji reached out and seized hold of both Jazz's hands in her own worn-out ones. She held on tight and stared with her big soft eyes into Jazz's face. It was scary. It felt as though she could see through Jazz's eyes and deep into her brain.

Jazz tried to pull away. She looked up at the clear sky, then down at the stone ground. The old woman kept on holding.

'Leave off staring at me that way,' said Jazz. 'Sure, my two eyes are green. Green as Galway, so Bridie says. Now will you give over? You're not my own mother so you canna tell me off.'

Oldest Auntiji began another long ramble.

'How am I meant to know what you're blethering about?' Jazz said, snatching her hands away.

Then she caught the sound of 'Rajinder'. She was talking about him.

Had he, Jazz wondered, looked like his mother, with those same brown eyes? And could that be why Jazz's own eyes were so sad and big?

The old woman was missing most of her teeth. Would Jazz, too, be missing as many teeth when she was as old as this very old grandmother?

Oldest Auntiji started talking slowly and clearly in Punjabi, just like the old man telling Jazz to write the letter. It wasn't one of her mumble-moans. This time it sounded as though she was telling a story.

But whatever it was she was saying, there wasn't another word of it apart from 'Rajinder' that Jazz could follow.

So what was he like? she wanted to ask. There's things I have to know. Did he take sweet tea like you make it? Or did he like it bitter like Bridie makes it? Which of his brothers was his favourite?

Or perhaps its was something different she needed to ask. Like was he a wise man? Was he like one of the three kings at Christmas? Did angels tell him what to do?

'You stupid old bag!' Jazz said. 'Why can't you talk to me properly?'

Oldest Auntiji stopped telling her story, readjusted her *dupatta* and got back to the chapattis.

Jazz said, 'The trouble with this poor old granny here is no one ever lets her have any fun, isn't that so, old Nan? In Scotland we take care of our old folks. We sing and dance for them. Like this.'

Jazz began to skip round and round Oldest Auntiji, singing at the top of her voice.

'Oh ye canna shove your granny off the bus! Oh ye canna shove your granny, cos she's your mammy's mammy, no ye canna shove your granny off the bus!'

And each time she went round Oldest Auntiji, she flicked at her *dupatta* so it nearly came off.

'Go on, Granny, laugh! That's what you're supposed to do. It's meant to be a funny song.'

The people in the courtyard stopped what they were doing and stared. So Jazz began another verse, even louder.

'Ye can shove your other granny, cos she's your dadda's mammy, but ye canna shove this granny off the bus,' she chanted, while Oldest Auntiji sat there on her haunches, not moving. She looked as though she was going to cry.

'Come on, you folks, will you no join in my wee singsong to cheer up the old besom?'

Jazz skipped so fast she was nearly falling over her legs with excitement, just like they did in the playground. But here the bystanders weren't laughing. They weren't even smiling. They were stony-faced.

'Och, you stupid folk, you think I'm useless, don't you? I'll show you. You haven't seen anything yet.'

The younger aunts were gathering into a huddle, talking to each other in low fierce voices. They sounded angry.

One of them called something to Jazz.

'Canna understand you, canna understand!' Jazz crowed back and she picked up a stick from the wood pile. She meant to poke the fire with it, to stir it into a blaze. But she was skipping so fast that she missed the embers and poked Oldest Auntiji's bottom instead.

'Oops. Sorry, Old Gran. Just my bit of fun,' said Jazz, grinning.

It stirred Oldest Auntiji into life. She leaped to her unsteady feet, shaking her fists.

Jazz dropped the stick and darted across the courtyard,

kicking over a basket of vegetables, and then away up the brick steps. When she reached the flat rooftop she sat down and pretended to admire the view. A few moments later, Harjit appeared.

Jazz said, 'Och, is it not grand to be up here, breathing fresh air and enjoying the peace? It can be that stifling down below.'

Harjit grabbed Jazz's hand. 'Please, Sis, listen. This is grave. They have been thinking, how maybe you should be beaten, to make you obedient and submissive. They say if you are really a child of this family, then you must be treated as one.'

'Beat me?' Jazz grinned. For a moment, she thought it must be a joke.

'With a stick. They would take the same stick you used to beat Auntiji.'

'I did never beat her! I was trying to make her laugh. It was an accident. It only just touched her. All in good fun!'

Suddenly Jazz was frightened. She had been in fair fights with boys, but she had never been beaten. Bridie used to yell and scream a lot but had never hit her. At school, Mrs Macpherson used to threaten to shake the living daylights out of the class if they were rowdy but it was only words. She never did it.

Here, she felt, they probably meant it.

'Beat me, would they? Och no, they'll soon see what happens to them if they try that. Just let them dare! I shall beat them back. And I am very strong and a great fighter.'

'They are waiting to discuss it when the uncles return. Please stay here, Sister, quietly. And I will plead for you. Then I will call you when it is safe for you to come down and apologise.'

Harjit hurried back down the steps.

Come down? thought Jazz, I'll no come down there, never, never. I've had it up to *here* with them! I'm leaving. *Then* they'll be sorry.

As soon as Harjit had gone, Jazz crossed the wooden causeway to the next rooftop, and the next, till she reached another flight of broken steps that led halfway down to the ground. From there she jumped onto the straw roof of a shed, and slid the rest of the way.

She landed in one of the narrow alleys. The only other creature in sight was the hairless dog, chewing something. When it saw Jazz, it crept away with its tail down.

Jazz trotted quickly off the other way towards the open fields. She wouldn't get like that silly old woman, too busy to have time to get out and enjoy herself.

8

Boggarts and Banshees

Jazz saw people crouched on wide dusty fields with baskets. They were gathering potatoes. But, unlike Harjit and the girls, they didn't bother with Jazz. So she kept on walking.

She saw scarlet blossoms glowing on a bush, every bit as bright as berries on a rowan tree, and tiny white flowers in the wayside grass as bonny as dog roses beside the Kelvin.

It was just like Mrs Macpherson used to say. There's nothing like a wheesh of fresh air to shift a black dog off your back.

Harjit was right, too. It was indeed fine out here among the fields. Not fine like the open countryside of Scotland was fine, all wild with scudding clouds and woolly sheep and bent-over trees, but fine enough all the same in a different way. Here, every field was tidy. There was hardly any space of land that was not being used for something. And the trees were tidy too, not bent over by the wind but in neat shady lines and comfortable clusters.

Jazz felt she had probably walked for about twenty miles and she began to feel quite hungry. If there'd been a chippie handy, she'd have popped in for a fifty-pence-worth of hot chips with a sprinkle of salt and a splash of vinegar.

The sun was beginning to go down.

In the distance, she saw the shape of three women walking. They were in single file because the track was narrow. Jazz realised she'd better catch up with them or she'd be alone out here. But by the time she'd reached the track that she thought they'd been on, they'd quite disappeared. Perhaps they hadn't really been there.

Further away she saw a bullock cart hurrying for home.

This time she ran fast, right across a field of low pea plants. But a bullock hurrying for home goes faster than a running girl. She lost sight of that too.

The light faded to dusty pink. Even the trees in the dusk looked pink. Jazz grew angry with the family. They might at least come out and look for her. They were as bad as Bridie, who didn't care one way or the other whether Jazz was in watching telly or out playing down the street.

The parrots disappeared into the shadows of the trees. It grew dark faster than Jazz expected. It was night and there was no reassuring phone box to go into and dial 999.

The moon came over the trees, round as a perfect chapatti baking on the hot iron plate. But there was no useful orange glow of street lights, or flashing neons, to lead her to safety.

But Jazz refused to be afraid of the night. Those goblins and leprechauns, fairies and pookas, banshees and boggarts with which Bridie tried to frighten her, did not know how to travel from one continent to another, not like Jazz did. They would still be back there in the dark recess at the bottom of the tenement stairwell.

Once upon a time, Harjit had informed her, India had been not one country but many kingdoms at war with one another. There had been thugs and robbers, brigands and revolutionaries who rushed about killing each other. Jazz wondered if there were still some left, lurking in the dark.

The faster Jazz hurried, the more uncertain she was which way to go.

She was hot and thirsty from running along so many dusty tracks. If only there was a corner shop she could pop into and get a can of fizzy Irn-Bru and ask the way.

There was water in the ditch beside the track. It was scarcely even trickling and you weren't supposed to drink water from anywhere except a tap or a pump, unless it had been boiled. But it must be all right. Harjit was always going on about how brilliant the water was round here.

Jazz knelt down and scooped up a handful.

At least she wasn't thirsy any more. Just lost. She was also very tired. She heard the voice of the holy man reading from the holy book, or thought she did. So it must soon be morning. But, even with the loudspeakers, the voice sounded faint and far away. Perhaps it was only a dog barking or frogs croaking.

She came to a small building in a clump of trees. The whitewashed walls showed up in the moonlight. There was no door, just an opening and a sloping roof. At first, Jazz thought it must be a farm shelter but there were no animals inside and the smooth floor was clean of animal dung.

Jazz remembered the Greenock Venture Scouts, reported on the telly news. They were lost in a blizzard on Ben Nevis. When they were rescued, they were praised for having gone into a stone bothy and stayed put all night instead of wandering about in the snow and dark.

So that's what I'm doing, Jazz thought to herself. Playing safe. Even so, it felt a wee bit like going into someone's private home without an invitation, especially when she saw in the pale light that there was food set out.

Two bananas, a round-shaped fruit that might have been an orange or an apple and a heap of corn snacks had been carefully arranged on a large leaf with some flowers. It was almost as though someone had been expecting a visitor and had put the food ready.

Perhaps those angels had at last bothered to watch out for her?

At the same time, she knew she shouldn't eat anything that had not been cooked specially. Miss MacFadyen had told her that. They learned that in school too, about never accepting food from people you didn't know. But she really was very hungry.

The banana was horrible and sloppy, so rotten it was almost liquid. The corn snacks tasted mouldy. Perhaps the food hadn't been left by guardian angels but by boggarts or banshees.

Jazz lay down, pulling her Kool Kats sweatshirt over her head so that if boggarts or banshees were after her, at least she wouldn't see them coming.

'Good night, God bless. Angels guard you while you rest,' she whispered many times over.

It was Harjit who found her first.

Instead of being cross, she hugged her tight.

'Oh, Sisterji! You are safe! We were so worried for you.'

'Well, you didn't need to be,' snapped Jazz, shivering from fear and relief.

Surinder, Kuldeep and Pritpal also emerged from the shadows. They crowded round, patting her and stroking her hands and her hair.

Then they all started crying. The only way to stop them was to let them hold her hands as they led the way back.

'Were you not afraid?' Harjit asked. 'To be all alone in that place?'

'It's what you're meant to do when you're lost,' said Jazz firmly. 'Find a good little hut to shelter in.' It was too difficult to explain about the Venture Scouts lost on Ben Nevis.

Harjit said in a whisper, 'No, Sis. That was not any hut. That was a holy man's shrine.'

'What d'you mean?'

'His burial place, sacred and special, so that people can remember him and think about him. And feel holy. On feast days, some of the older women leave food and offerings for him.'

'If he's dead, he can't eat it.'

'It is not for eating. It would be horrible to eat. They leave it there so long. It is symbolic.'

Jazz said nothing about how she had eaten some of the food she'd found. There was a word for what she'd done. It was even worse than teasing an old woman. Mrs Macpherson had explained about it once, when she was talking about people who sprayed red paint on Jewish gravestones.

'It's called sacrilege, children,' she had said.

Harjit said, 'At home, they do not know you have gone. I let them believe you had come down from the roof and were in the room, offering your prayers for mercy to God. But were you so afraid that you must run away? They would not beat you too hard.'

'Who says I was afraid? I just went out for air.'

But even while she was pretending to be brave, Jazz kept close to Harjit. She didn't want to go getting lost again.

As they hurried through the dark, Harjit said, 'Maybe they will decide not to beat you after all, for Kuldeep told them the fault was also with us, your cousins, for not taking better care of you. We should have shown you what are our customs.'

When they reached the courtyard, the girls helped Jazz creep in without being noticed while they themselves did a lot of giggling.

Once she was safely under the quilt, shivering with fear and cold, Jazz heard the girls being severely scolded by all the adults for having dared go out after dark.

Jazz wondered if they, too, would all be beaten next day.

9

Sick as a Dog

Jazz did not know she was falling ill. She only knew that she woke in the deep part of night feeling afraid. But it wasn't about whether or not she was going to be punished.

It was because, somewhere, she was hurting. But where? Was it her back? Or her head? Or her legs? She felt like one of those heavy buffaloes that had been made to pull a waggon that was too heavy.

She was too hot as well.

She threw off Aunty's cotton quilt, then she was shivering with cold and groped to find it again.

Then the cramps gripped her and she needed to get out to the toilet hut quickly. She had to step over her sleeping cousins in the dark and find her way to the bolted door. At night, it was bolted from the inside in case a robber climbed into the courtyard and the bald dog didn't hear. Jazz had to feel around for the metal bolt.

In daylight, the courtyard was friendly enough. Now it was like a wide dangerous swamp with moonlight shadows moving. Or perhaps that was a robber with a gleaming scimitar hiding. Or a gang of rats.

Somewhere, a dog howled. Or perhaps it was a jackal laughing. Then, into the blacker than black of the toilet.

After she had crouched over the hole, Jazz had to cross the dark courtyard to the pump with the bucket to fill it and return it. Then, exhausted, she returned to bed and rebolted the door.

She tried to sleep. Twice more, then a fourth time, then a fifth and a sixth time she had to get up and cross the courtyard. She was no longer afraid of robbers or jackals, only of not reaching the hut in time.

After each visit, she felt worse, not better. She wondered, was she being punished by the angels for being so cruel to Oldest Auntiji?

She wanted the holy readings to start. That would mean someone was awake, and daytime was only two more hours away.

Everything was silent. Even the jackal had gone quiet.

Jazz peered into the darkness for the angels that were supposed to guard her. Why did they have to be invisible? Bridie had lied and they were not there at all. Bridie was like that.

Now Jazz was on fire. She needed water to drink. But she was too feeble to stagger yet again across the yard to the pump.

'Bridie,' she whispered. 'Will you no come and help me, please? I will never cross you again. Come and get me.'

Harjit turned in her sleep and half woke. 'Sisterji?' she said.

'Want some water,' said Jazz.

'What is it? Are you sick?'

Jazz shook her head. 'No, no, no.' She didn't want to be sick.

Her bones ached. The ceiling wheeched round above her head.

Harjit fetched some water in a tin beaker.

It was so good and cold and wet.

Jazz began falling down a black deep well. She never reached the bottom but went on tumbling through a dark mist.

She thought she might have died. But she could not see Michael, nor any of the other blessed saints who, so Bridie sometimes said, would be waiting for her, though only if she was a good girl.

She thought of the number of times she had screamed at

Bridie how much she hated her, how she had called her a tumshie, a besom, an old cuddy. She thought of that time she had bitten Alasdair Baxter's hand just for something to do, and she guessed she was not often good in the way Bridie meant.

Then someone gave her something to drink and she knew that she could not be dead, but perhaps quite ill.

She wondered how soon she would die and when she did, what they would do with her. Would they give her a decent procession nearly a mile long, like the one they'd watched in Galway? Or would they just pretend she'd never existed?

Would Bridie miss her and cry for ever?

'Am I going to die?' she asked the person who held the beaker of water for her to drink from.

'No, Sister. You have a fever. By tomorrow you will be well and arguing with us once more.'

But soon Jazz could no longer sit up to moan that she was going to die. She guessed she must be getting worse when, one after another, the aunts came to inspect her, then stood in the doorway discussing what to do.

The cousins took turns to sit beside her, cooling her with a big fan, and one of the aunties brought Jazz a special kind of tea.

'It is ginger in buttermilk to soothe the stomach,' said Harjit. 'Go on, try please.'

Jazz swallowed it down and soon sicked it up. She didn't get better. Then another aunty brought another kind of tea.

'It is cardamom and cloves with water and honey,' explained Harjit.

Oldest Auntiji brought the most disgusting of all which, Harjit said, was *shatavi* and licorice.

Jazz sicked them all up.

Finally a stranger in white came, bringing yet another mixture.

'Do not be afraid. She is our medicine woman who brings natural healing,' said Harjit. 'So please try to sip her beverage. You are very fortunate. She comes to important people.'

Jazz was ill all the next night too, only she didn't know if it was night or day.

She dreamed that she was a flying jackal galloping through the sky only to meet a flock of blue parrots and some angry yellow angels who were flying in the opposite direction.

In the morning two of the aunts went out to the fields to fetch one of the uncles who ran home to borrow the neighbour's motor-scooter. Uncle and the neighbour rode to the government clinic in town. There, they waited in line with many other men and women, children and babies.

When it was finally their turn, the nurse on duty said, 'It's no good if the child isn't here. How can we treat her if she isn't here?'

'But she's too ill to bring on the scooter.'

'Then you must find another way,' the nurse told them. 'But first give her the salt and sugar mixture.'

Uncle and the neighbour didn't know what it was. 'A pinchful of salt, a spoonful of sugar, in a litre of water. She must drink it ever hour.'

Uncle and the neighbour went to the railway station and hired a taxi. The taxi man wasn't used to going out into the countryside. He didn't know the way to any of the villages. So the two men on the scooter rode in front, showing the way. The taxi followed.

Jazz knew none of this. It was only later when Harjit was telling her things, as usual, that she began to remember being rolled up in the cotton quilt, carried out and laid on the back seat of the taxi.

Harjit told her how excited the small children had been to see the black car, with the sign TAXI stuck in the windscreen, bumping along the track with the scooter just ahead. And how they crowded around to watch Jazz being carried out, limp and moaning, to be transported away in a cloud of dust.

'And when they reached the clinic, because they could see you were a very important English person,' Harjit said later, 'they put you in a small room on your own.'

'I'm no English!' said Jazz. 'I'm from Scotland.' It was irritating how Harjit still could not tell the difference.

'Yes, because they could see you are a foreigner,' Harjit agreed.

'And how do you know all this?' Jazz said. 'When you weren't even there?' She was annoyed to have Harjit telling her things even about herself.

Being in a room on her own made little difference to Jazz, though a lot of difference, Harjit explained, to the family.

'A single room is of greater cost to the family,' she said. 'But it would bring so much dishonour on the heads of the uncles if you were to perish for lack of care.'

As Jazz began to feel stronger, she felt lonely in the single room. She sat up and saw how she was not really alone. A crowd of scraggy children were standing in the doorway, staring curiously at her. When they saw she was awake, they said, 'Hi, hi, hi, English? Hello?' just like the little boys in the village.

Jazz cussed them but they did not understand.

'Will you no go away and leave me in peace!' she shrieked.

They fled and Jazz was lonelier than before.

However, she got to view the other patients when everybody's beds were lifted outside so that the sweepers could come round with their buckets and twig brooms to sluice over the floors and walls. While they swished water into all the corners to flush out germs and microbes, cockroaches and crumbs, the beds with sick bodies still in them were lined up in two rows in a flower garden beneath the shady trees. Patients who were well enough chatted to one another and even tried to chat to Jazz.

Jazz turned on her side and looked at the way the dappled sun fell through the leaves on to the bed quilt. She sobbed for Bridie and for the dirty, empty, cold flat on the fourth floor.

And she wept for the new girl in Class 6 with the goofy teeth. And she cried for those cousins in Ireland whose names she couldn't even remember now. And, to her own surprise, she even sniffed a little bit for Oldest Auntiji, though she couldn't understand why she was wasting her tears on an old woman with hardly any teeth.

10

The Din of a Greetin Teenie

By midday when the sun was high and the air as hot as a bread oven, the beds were lifted back into the blue shade of the rooms. Everybody slept. Most patients had people from their own families staying with them to take care of them and they too slept, on their mats, on the floor beside the beds.

Jazz had never stayed in a hospital before, except that first time at the Queen Mother's to get herself born. But that was so far back she couldn't remember and every time she asked, Bridie told a different tale. However, Jazz felt right sure that when Angus was carried off to the Western Infirmary with a cracked kneebone, it had not been his family but the nurses who'd cared for him. His mother just sat on a chair beside his bed, reading magazines.

Here, Jazz had no family. And she was in a room on her own. And anyway, sleeping in the afternoon was silly. 'Only weans and wimps sleep in the afternoon.'

So instead of sleeping, she sobbed without tears, but loud enough for all to hear.

There were plenty of other sick children whimpering. And at first, not a lot happened, apart from getting a hoarse throat and some small boys gathering in the doorway and calling, 'Hi, hi, hi!'

Jazz was thinking about giving up on the sobbing and moving on to gasping, roaring and keening when a woman appeared on the verandah outside the room and shooed away the small boys.

'Hold your wheesht! Will you no stop your deaving noise?'

The woman poked her head round the window blinds. She

wore a white doctor's coat over her *salvar kameez*, and a white *dupatta* over red curly hair. She had staring blue eyes, the colour of Loch Katrine on a midsummer day. She was talking in a way that Jazz understood all too well.

It was angry language.

'There's been nocht but wailing and greetin ever since they brought you in! We're all of us trauchled enough from overwork without the din of a greetin teenie.'

Nobody had spoken to Jazz like this for a long while. It took her breath away. She swallowed down the roar that she'd been about to release.

'So this is the gallus wee lassie who's been making all the rammy?' said the doctor sternly.

Jazz sank back onto the stripy mattress, trying to look as though she was too poorly to have created any disturbance at all, let alone a rammy.

'Och, you're enough to feart the banshees with all your wailing! And, so I hear, you've been no letting them lie easy in their beds back at hame?'

'Hame?' Jazz whispered. 'I dinna ken where is ma hame.'

'Aye, you know well enough who I mean. The folks in the village who brought you in.'

'They're no my folks!' Jazz spat like a feral cat.

'They've been caring like you were their own first-born son.'

Jazz closed her eyes and pretended she'd fallen asleep.

The angry doctor would have none of it. She came right in and sat firmly down on the edge of the metal bed.

'Och fegs, hen! Will you no consider for a moment. You travel alone halfway round the globe. A sight more than most lassies of your years would dare. But then, when all these kindly folks want to do is receive you into their hearth, you stick your stubborn heels in. They can only do it when you're willing too.'

Jazz wanted to tell her to stop her blether. That's what she'd have told Bridie. But she had not the courage. Those blue eyes set in a freckled face looked right into her. They could see everything inside her, just like the X-ray film looking into Angus's knee.

'They paid a bonny penny to bring you over here. And you've no right to taunt them so. You've to show these couthie folks you're someone to respect for all their trouble. Och, if you'd only started out that way! They say it's never too late to make amends, but I have my doubts.'

Cautiously, Jazz dared say, 'You're no understanding how it is. They're that strange.'

'Strange?' said the doctor. 'How so?'

'Everything they do is that different from what I was expecting.'

'Aye, so it is. And that's the joy in it. Would you be wanting to travel all this way to find everything just the same as what you came from?'

'And they want *me* to be different too,' Jazz whined.

The doctor snorted angrily. 'And I should hope so too, right different from the way you have been. Och my, they are that tolerant folk, keeping their hearts open for you. I'm telling you, if you'd been sent as one of *my* long-lost cousins, I'd have put you right back on the next flight away. And that's no joke.'

Two nurses and a technician came scurrying along the verandah calling out for Dr Elspeth.

She got up. 'I must be on my way to see to those folks who are still right poorly. So you take your nap and have a wee think.' She patted Jazz's hand in a way that was friendly enough, but also quite firm, rather like Mrs Macpherson. Jazz understood that language too. It said, 'Dinna you footer wi' me or you'll know what's coming!'

Fierce Dr Elspeth looked in on Jazz regularly, popping her curly head round the window and smiling, or wagging a bossy finger and waving her stethoscope. At first, Jazz didn't do much back. But after a while she had enough strength to lift her head and snarl. Each time, Dr Elspeth ignored the bad temper and chatted brightly, as though Jazz was listening.

'Did you know what Scots and Sikhs have in common? Grand travellers, the lot of them. Just as you've come over here from Scotland, so there's Sikh people travelling the world over.'

Jazz remembered how Harjit had said something fairly similar.

'They say there's more Sikhs spread around the world,' said Dr Elspeth, 'than are left living in the whole of the Punjab. Canada, Britain, Australia, Singapore. Just like the Scots, more of them travelling around than there are in the whole of Scotland from Wick down to St Abbs.'

'I do not care for your tales,' said Jazz. 'You tire me out.'

The visits left Jazz pooped. And after that, the tears began to pour from her eyes. She tried to stifle them. But they kept on coming. She buried herself in the darkness under the quilt as though she were a dead body under the turf.

Perhaps it would have been better for everyone if she had died and gone to the Land o' the Leal to meet St Michael. Then she'd have caused no more stushie to anyone, none to Mrs Macpherson, nor to Miss MacFadyen, nor to the couthie couple with their goldfish, nor been a bother to bossy Harjit, and especially not been a tyrant to Oldest Auntiji.

Jazz remembered how, in a fit of stushie, she had once, or more likely at least twice, and probably half a dozen times, screamed at Bridie that she wished she'd never been born, that she wished she were dead.

'And I wish the same to you!' Bridie had screeched back, but immediately after, had begun to cry. 'No, no, no! I never meant it.'

Jazz just yelled, 'Well, that's no making me change my mind!'

But later, in the night, Jazz had had to creep across the cold lino and up into Bridie's bed where she snuggled up and clung to Bridie's back like she was a drowning puppy in a fast-flowing river.

Now, under the quilt in this strange-lumpy bed, with no one to cling to, or to talk to, or to tell her make-up stories of summers in Galway, she imagined what it might feel like to have once had a child and to have lost that child, not just for a while when she went travelling across the world, but for ever when she went to heaven.

Jazz thought about Oldest Auntiji with her big brown eyes and missing her best teeth. She was not a cruel witch, but a sad, worn-out, old carline, just like you might see down on Paddy's Market sorting through second-hand curtains. Whenever they saw a woman like that, Bridie used to say, 'Go on, Jazz, give her a penny, for that might be me one of these days.'

And even if the old person wasn't begging, Bridie'd give her enough for a cup of tea.

Jazz thought how Oldest Auntiji had been working her whole life away, ever since she married at fourteen. Jazz also thought of Oldest Auntiji losing too many of her children whom she'd never see again.

Jazz thought of where she'd come from, where they had a television with four channels, indoor water you didn't have to pump up, a flushing toilet, a cooker that worked with a switch instead of cow dung, and shops where they could buy ready-made chapattis.

How much, Jazz wondered, did Oldest Auntiji miss her son Rajinder? Was it as much as Jazz had missed the paper dolly that got burned up? Or was it a different kind of missing? Did Oldest Auntiji think about her lost children every day or was she too busy? And how could she think properly about Rajinder when she'd never even seen the place where he'd lived?

Oldest Auntiji knew nothing about the Clydeside Express-way, nor about underground trains. Oldest Auntiji had never even seen the sea, nor walked down Sauchiehall Street and looked at the shops. She had never seen the fireworks outside the Winter Gardens.

Jazz knew about things. So Jazz must be strong. She must smile at the old lady. She must accept the sweeties she was offered.

Maybe it was already too late. Maybe when Jazz left this clinic, she would not be going back to the family. Maybe they'd send her to New Delhi and onto a flight home, just like Dr Elspeth said she'd have done if she'd had to put up with such a right greetin teenie.

How then would Jazz explain it when she got back? She could already hear Angus McLeod tearing round the playground yelling out to everyone, 'They sent her back! They sent her back!' And then Jamie taking up the cry, 'Jaswinder is a feartie! Jaswinder is a feartie!'

A gentle hand through the quilt shook Jazz awake. It was a woman whose sari was edged with a shimmery silver thread which caught the light so that, for just a moment, Jazz thought she was looking at a pretty tinsel angel off the top of a Christmas tree.

'Miss, miss,' she said. 'Please wake now. I am the dietician for the clinic. I have to speak with you. The physician tells us you must try to eat solid foods once more. Here in the clinic we provide all patients with two good meals a day. But I am regretful. We are not a rich clinic. We have only our own food here. We have not your American-type food.'

'But I'm no American,' said Jazz.

'Excuse me. Forgive me. I wish to say, it is European food we do not have either. Hamburger. Fish finger. Fried potato chip.'

Jazz had eaten nothing for a long time. She was still not sure if she would ever want to eat again.

'We offer curds and milk, and chapattis and dahl,' the shimmery dietician said. 'All is high quality but it is not your food.'

Jazz thought about the chips she could not have, and she thought about the buffalo-milk curds. The thought of buffalo-milk curds made her feel like being sick again.

She said, in a very tiny voice, 'Och, that's grand. I'll eat whatever comes my way. And may the Lord make me truly grateful for every cup and plateful.' That's what they used to say round the big table at Bridie's folks' place.

The meal was brought round on a wooden truck pulled by two men. Jazz saw the chapattis, hundreds of them, heaped in a great rush basket, keeping warm under a green cloth. She watched the dahl ladled out from a bucket. She did her best to seem eager. She ate a corner of her chapatti and drank a mouthful of curds.

To her surprise, two of the young aunties turned up. She wanted to be able to tell them how their chapattis were better than the ones here. But Harjit was not there to translate.

The aunts greeted her, smiled and explained something.

Jazz wondered what they wanted.

They fetched water from the pump in the centre of the clinic grounds, warmed it over a fire outside where other families were also heating water. They brought it into Jazz's room in a tin bowl. Jazz wondered if they were going to start making soup.

Jazz realised the aunties had come to look after her, just like the other patients' families were doing. They undressed Jazz, and they washed her as gently as though she were a newborn baby. As they patted and dried her, they chatted cheerfully to each other over her, almost as though she really were a tiny wean who could not understand, yet knew it was being cared for. It was very strange.

Carefully, they re-dressed her in a clean cotton shift with embroidery down the front that looked like one of Pritpal's. They changed the sheet on the bed. They tucked Jazz under the quilt.

They were just leaving when Jazz remembered what she had to do. Quickly, before they left, she sat up, placed her hands together, and bowed her head.

'*Sat sri akal*,' she said to each of the aunties in turn.

Jazz had no idea what it meant. But it was what they said to each other all the time.

The two aunties stared at Jazz in astonishment, rather as though a bald dog or a green parrot had suddenly spoken like a human.

Then they laughed.

'*Sat sri akal,*' they replied, then came over and each gave Jazz a quick tight hug just like Bridie used to.

Then they waved and left.

The sun had already gone down. Jazz wondered how they were going to get home. 'Will you be all right?' she wanted to ask.

But of course they wouldn't have understood what she was blethering about.

11

High Tea

It was already dark, with the mosquito screens hooked securely over the windows and night insects buzzing around the lamps on the verandah, when Dr Elspeth came again to see Jazz.

'And how is our gallus wee tyrant this evening?' she asked.

She carried a tray. Jazz thought it must be time for more medicine. But Dr Elspeth wasn't wearing her doctor's coat, just her blue *salvar kameez*

She said, 'We've had the results of the tests. And you're well on the road to recovery. But there's another wee sickness we've only just identified.'

Dr Elspeth had already told Jazz she'd had dysentery, though whether from drinking dirty water or from the mouldy fruit at the holy man's shrine, they could not tell. Either way, Jazz promised never again to drink from stagnant pools nor to help herself to food that wasn't hers to take.

'I'm feeling just grand now,' said Jazz, smiling eagerly to demonstrate how healthy she was. 'Really fine.' She didn't want any more medicines which were disgusting to take and, she realised, costly to the family.

'Och, that's as maybe, my dear,' said Dr Elspeth. 'But my investigations suggest you may be suffering from yet another sickness.'

She set down her tray on the bed. On it was a dainty china teapot, a pair of cups with saucers and a round tin printed with a tartan pattern and some purple thistles. It looked like a very old, slightly rusty, biscuit tin.

'They call it homesickness. There's no permanent cure but

I believe I may have a partial cure right here. Now, do you care for Scottish baking, by any chance? It so happens there's a finger or two of shortbread left.'

She poured the tea and opened up the tin. 'Och my, and a wee piece of the Abernethy farl in here too. I've been waiting for the right moment to share it with someone who understands the importance of Scottish baking.'

'I'm partly a Paddy.'

'So may the Irish part of you never enjoy home baking?'

'Aye, Bridie bakes a grand soda bread.'

Dr Elspeth said in a serious voice, 'The problem with identifying homesickness is that it affects all folk differently. There's some travel the whole globe over, and feel never a twinge. Others move only to the next street and are suffering for the rest of their lives. I'm telling you, I cried a full three months when I first left home.'

The idea of someone as grown-up as a doctor crying was silly.

Jazz said, 'How can I be homesick when I dinna ken which home I'm to be sick about? I dinna belong anywhere. I'm no even half and half, just a load of things muddled up. Bridie wants me to be Irish. I thought I belonged to Glasgow but they wouldna let me.'

'Who wouldn't let you?'

'The others.'

'Who's that? Can you tell me?'

Jazz told Dr Elspeth about the children at school who laughed at her, calling her a Paki.

'When I tell them I canna be, for my mother's from Galway, they call me a Paddy. And when I say I dinna wanna be a Paddy, they call me a Proddie. So after that, I always have to fight them.'

She did not mention how she herself liked to name call Clarence Lo a Chinky-Chinaman-likey-eatey-fried-dog, and he never fought back, just walked away with his nose in the air.

Nor did she mention how, when she picked a fight, she always won. That was not the sort of thing to impress a doctor.

Dr Elspeth's tea tasted strange and thin without condensed milk and cardamom spice.

'So you would let these *other* children decide for you such an important thing in your life?' said Dr Elspeth. 'And what is wrong with belonging to two places?'

'Because you canna do that,' said Jazz. 'It's not permitted.'

Dr Elspeth said, 'First I heard of it! I've belonged in at least two places for years. Born in Dundee and belonged there, school in Edinburgh, belonged there too. Studied in Perth. And now I've been here for twenty years. So I reckon I belong here. But those other places are mine too. No one can take them from me.'

Jazz shrugged. It was odd, but trying to remember what St Mungo's Road looked like was growing difficult. Like the memory of what Rajinder looked like, it had faded.

'The first time I went back to Scotland I was like you, none too sure where I belonged. Over here, they called me the Scottish lady. Over there, they asked why I spoke like an Indian. These days, I know exactly who I am. I'm a Haggis-Indian. There are not so very many of us but we are strong as elephants. And that suits me fine.'

'So you belong to several places at once?' said Jazz.

'Aye. And that makes me not divided but doubled. You give it a try. Just to see if it fits you the same way. Now, why not take a taste of that shortbread, baked by my own sister Morag, and tell me what you think.'

Jazz was not hungry, but she gave it a nibble and tried to look as though she was enjoying it. She wondered what Angus McLeod would say about the Haggis-Indians. Would he jeer, or start a fight, or might he want to be one too?

Jazz wanted to tell Elspeth about Rajinder's family, about how none of it had turned out like she'd expected. It wasn't the sort of thing she could have told a grown-up like Mrs

Macpherson, let alone Miss MacFadyen. But somehow Dr Elspeth, even if she was stern, seemed safe.

'See, I was hoping all along as maybe I'd find a bit of Rajinder. But there's none of him here, even less than back home. But they still want me to be like a proper Indian girl. Inside of me, I know I'm still me, who I was. And I did no think on them being that poor. Except they're no really so poor, not in the way we think of poor in Glasgow.'

Dr Elspeth nodded as though she understood.

'And the oldest Auntiji, she's my grandma, she's no one wee bit like my friend Jennie's Nan. Another thing that's turned out wrong, my friend Jennie told me I was some kind of royalty.'

'Then your friend is not so far off the truth. Every Sikh woman is a princess, every Sikh girl too. That's the meaning of their name, Kaur. Princess.'

Jazz wondered what Jennie Stewart would make of that. And as for Angus, would it make him hopping mad?

Dr Elspeth said, 'And the middle name for Sikh men is Singh.'

'Everybody knows that. It was Rajinder's name too.'

'And does everybody know it means "lion"?'

'A lion?' Jazz was disappointed. If she could be a princess of sorts, she would have liked to have discovered that Rajinder had indeed been a king, like one of the wise men at Christmas. 'Just a lion? That's not much. I don't know what Jennie'll think.'

'Do you only worry about what your friends have to say? Do you never make up your own mind?' asked Dr Elspeth. 'A lion is strong and brave and a fighter to the end.'

Jazz said, 'And may a girl be as brave as a lion too? Do you think it could be true, what you said yesterday, how it was brave to come round the world on my own?'

Dr Elspeth thought for a moment, then she said, 'I did the same thing myself, and that seemed like the bravest thing I'd ever done. So if it was brave of me twenty years ago, it must be brave of you now. Or else I'm a drunken Dutchman.'

Jazz said, 'Rajinder went to Scotland on his own. And he didna speak a word of the language and had no family to stay with.'

'Then he was couragous as a lion.'

Jazz wanted to tell Dr Elspeth something else important, not about Rajinder's people but about Bridie.

'She's my mother. And she's no good. She's that untrustworthy. See, she was always telling me how I must pray to the angels to take care of me when I came over here and I'd be all right. But they didna help me. So she's a liar.'

Instead of agreeing, Dr Elspeth asked, 'And what would an angel look like?'

Jazz said crossly, 'They don't look like anything, of course, because they're not true. And even if they were, you wouldna get them here. Sikhs don't have angels. Harjit told me.'

'Is that so? said Dr Elspeth, smiling. 'All these years here, and I thought I had seen so many. For what are angels other than kind folks who look out for other people?'

Next morning, one of the young aunties arrived at the clinic with one of the young uncles and the next-door neighbour's motor-scooter to take Jazz home.

Jazz wanted to say goodbye to Dr Elspeth but didn't know how to find her. So she got a scrap of paper from the dietician and wrote a note. She left it on the bed. She hoped someone who could read English would find it. It said,

> To pass on to the Haggis-Indian Doctor.
>> Thank you for geting me beter. And helping me be a Haggis-Indian too. Now I will always be.
>> Love from Jaswinder.

She wanted to write 'Sat sri akal', but she didn't know how to spell it so she added, 'And Happy Xmas for next year if I don't see you agin' instead.

86

The aunty lifted Jazz up onto the pillion seat of the motor-scooter behind the uncle, then climbed on as well.

Back in Glasgow, you weren't allowed to ride three on a scooter. But this wasn't Glasgow. Like Dr Elspeth said, you shouldn't go halfway round the world and expect to find things the same.

They passed another scooter with four people piled on, as well as some hens in a basket.

After the quiet of the clinic courtyard, the busy high road was alarming. Even though she supposed she was better, Jazz felt dizzy and exhausted by the time they reached home.

In the courtyard, on the shady side, the *charpoi* day-bed was ready for her to lie on, heaped with cushions. Jazz was greeted with smiles and the neighbours' children grinned and stared just as they had on the day she'd first arrived.

Harjit said, 'This is because all are joyful that you return to us in health.'

The person who welcomed her most keenly was Oldest Auntiji. But instead of greeting her their way, eyes down, palms together, she flung her sturdy old arms right round Jazz and moaned to herself as though in a trance while rocking Jazz from side to side. It was like a hug from an elephant. The moaning was a name.

'Jaswinder, Jaswinder,' she crooned.

Then she let Jazz go, blew her nose on the corner of her *dupatta* and went back to the cooking corner.

Harjit said, 'Auntiji missed you.'

Jazz said, 'Yes, I know.'

'She missed you more than anybody else. She was most worried about you. She is glad you are back.'

'Yes,' said Jazz. 'I know that too.'

All that day, nobody asked Jazz to do anything to help. Instead, the girls gave her presents.

There were coloured glass bangles like they wore which tinkled as you moved, a notebook with a patterned cover, a spray of white frangipani, a tiny bottle of pink rosewater.

'These gifts are to aid your recovery,' explained Harjit as she dabbed Jazz's forehead with the rosewater to refresh her and squeezed the palm of Jazz's hand to fit the bangles on.

Jazz was so spoiled that she didn't at first notice that Fat Lazy Spoiled Aunt was no longer using the *charpoi*.

Harjit said, 'We expect Aunty back from the nursing clinic this afternoon. And everybody will welcome her too, just as we welcome you.'

Fat Lazy Aunt returned by taxi. She no longer looked fat and lazy, but was a thin smiling aunty, shyly covering her face with her *dupatta* and holding another cousin in her arms.

'She's had a baby!' said Jazz, who was the only person to be surprised.

The newborn baby, one day old, was laid on the *charpoi* beside Jazz, under a white muslin cloth to keep the bright light from its eyes. Jazz lifted the corner of the cloth and took a peek. The baby was as tiny and perfect as a doll.

'Is it a boy or a girl?' she asked.

Thin smiling Aunty replied in Punjabi.

Harjit said, 'Aunty says to tell you that, in Sikh custom, the birth of any child, boy or girl, is always welcomed as a gift from God. For every child is born according to destiny and the will of God.'

12

Golden Day

'Come, look, Sis!' said Harjit. 'The bus is here.'

A gaudily-painted minibus with coloured fairy lights blinking round its windscreen and tinsel streamers fluttering round its top was backing up the alley outside the courtyard.

It was the same one which had fetched Jazz from the airport when she'd first arrived. A young uncle was behind the steering wheel. The little children rushed out to watch.

'See, Uncleji has hired it again!' said Harjit.

The toddlers clapped and laughed with excitement. But Jazz was worried sick.

Why was it here? Were they going to drive her to New Delhi today? Were they sending her away early?

Since her recovery, Jazz had helped every day with the dung patties without complaining. She helped prepare meals without skiving off. She greeted the older relations reverently every morning. She had not lost her temper with the little ones even when they teased her. She'd shared her chapatti with the miserable bald dog. She'd tried to look interested every time Harjit told her things about Diwali and Guru Nanak's birthday celebrations which she already knew.

Had it all been wasted effort? Had they none of them noticed how hard she'd been trying?

She and Harjit gathered the little ones out of the way of the minibus and ushered them back into the safety of the courtyard.

Anxiously, Jazz said, 'But it's no yet the time for me to leave. There's weeks and weeks left.'

Harjit laughed. 'No, no, no, little Sis! The vehicle is for

our excursion. Today we go to the Golden Temple. We are all excited. I have never been. Nor Surinder. And Auntiji has not visited since she was young. And your friend will be coming too.'

'My friend?' said Jazz. Who was her friend? She didn't have friends.

Harjit said, 'Uncleji sent a messenger to the esteemed doctor, in gratitude for saving your life.'

'Nobody saved my life. It was only runny tummy and I got better by myself,' Jazz started to say till she remembered to keep her lying blether to herself.

Harjit said, 'And your friend accepted Uncle's invitation and we will all be greatly honoured by her presence.'

The girls spent the morning giggling and getting ready. They tried on each other's clothes. They oiled and plaited each other's hair. They opened up their trinket chests and spread out their glass bangles, rings and necklaces to share with one another.

Jazz, watching, asked, 'This golden place, is it very posh?' The name sounded mysterious, making her think of Cinderella's coach filled up with golden nuggets.

Harjit replied, 'It is the most beautiful place in the world,' just as she said about everything.

Jazz said, 'How d'you know if you've no been there yet?'

'I have seen pictures. It is our most holy of holies, where the sacred book is kept. That is why we put on our best. There will be many visitors.'

Jazz wondered if it would be like going to Mass. But Harjit, who knew so much about most things, didn't know anything about Mass. She just said, 'Perhaps, Sis, you wish to borrow one of my pretty suits?'

'No thanks,' said Jazz. 'I've a best suit of my own. Been saving it for today.'

The pink *salvar kameez* was creased from being squashed at the bottom of the case. Jazz gave the tunic a vigorous shake and the girls helped smooth out the trousers. Jazz let them do her hair like theirs, and lend her some silver necklaces, and they admired her just as much as they had been admiring each other.

Nobody said anything about the pink being the colour of rhubarb. Jazz thought this might be because they didn't know what rhubarb was.

Kuldeep held up a little piece of broken mirror for Jazz to look at herself. She saw how, except for the colour of her eyes, she looked almost like one of them.

The boy cousins, too, had taken trouble to dress in fresh shirts and crisp bright turbans. The toddlers were in sparkly suits and dresses.

Dr Elspeth arrived by rickshaw. She was wearing a silvery-white *dupatta* with a silk *salvar kameez* almost the same colour as her eyes.

She greeted the older relations respectfully, hands together, eyes down. She greeted the younger uncles and aunts. She admired the new baby as though it was the first and most amazing baby she had seen in her life and she tucked a twenty-rupee note under the fold of its muslin cloth just as the neighbours had done. She brought a silver carton of pistachio sweetmeats for the family's picnic.

After the adults, she greeted each of the children, one by one.

'*Sat sri akal*,' she said.

'*Sat sri akal*,' each replied.

When it was Jazz's turn she said, '*Sat sri akal*, Jaswinder Kaur. Truth is eternal, Princess Jaswinder, Lord of Glory.'

Jazz lowered her head and her eyes, too scared to say a thing till Harjit nudged her in the ribs.

'*Sat sri akal*,' Jazz whispered. 'Truth is eternal.'

The greetings over, Dr Elspeth squatted with the aunties in the cooking corner to help prepare chapattis for the picnic.

She spoke Punjabi. This was irritating as Jazz couldn't understand. But from the way they were laughing together, it sounded like the usual chattering that the aunties did all day anyway. Jazz was surprised that a doctor, even a Haggis-Indian one, knew about gossiping and rolling chapatti dough as well as about diagnosing dysentery and saving lives.

It was a squash fitting everybody into the minibus. There were even more of them than when they'd come to the Mahatma Gandhi Airport.

They made frequent stops, first to ask the way when they got lost, then to let a flock of goats pass, then to pick up a cousin and his wife who were coming too. Then for glasses of tea and snacks from a roadside stall. Later, they had to stop abruptly when they came upon a hole in the road. They were stopped again at a military road-block, and to wait at a level crossing for a steam-engine to thunder by. Finally, when they reached the city of Amritsar, they stopped to ask the way to the Golden Temple.

They followed other pilgrims through the narrow streets. Jazz was glad of her cousins clustered round her, smiling, holding her hands, preventing her from being left behind. Or perhaps it was to prevent themselves from getting lost. The uncles, like shepherds, kept checking up that nobody was missing.

Jazz wasn't as nervous of the crowds as Oldest Auntiji. Even though she had two young aunties supporting her at each side, she looked terrified of the crowds.

At the entrance to the temple, the family queued up, women and girls in one line, men and boys in another, to remove their shoes or slippers, sandals or trainers, and hand them in to the shoe-keeper.

Outside the temple walls it was as noisy and bustling as Glasgow Fair. But within the grounds was like entering a different world. There was space and tranquillity.

They washed their bare feet, all together, Jazz and Dr Elspeth too, in a shallow foot-pool across the entrance.

'This is from respect for the holiest of holies,' explained Harjit. 'We must have clean feet and covered heads.' She tugged at Jazz's *dupatta* to pull it up better over her head.

The family went down the wide stone staircase. Numerous visitors were coming and going yet there seemed to be room for everybody without pushing or rushing.

People moved slowly like figures in a dream along the wide marble pavements surrounding the shimmering lake. Even little children seemed dreamy and contented as they skipped and hopped beside their mothers and fathers, aunties and uncles, sisters and cousins, grannies and grandfathers.

The one unhappy sound came from a small boy whose mother undressed him and dunked him into the holy water. But when she fished him out again, Jazz saw how he was laughing as well as spluttering.

Beyond the lake was the guru's garden, green and cool with fruit trees and flowering bushes. Visitors were lying on the lawns, relaxing beneath the trees.

The Golden Temple was in the middle of the shimmering lake.

Jazz's family crossed the bridge to reach it. The water on either side reflected the white buildings, the blue sky above and the rainbow-coloured clothing of the pilgrims.

'This is the pool of immortality,' Harjit said.

The golden roofs glowed in the burning sun as though they were on fire. The white marble walkways gleamed as cool as ice. There was a stillness and quietness which seemed far removed from the busy fields.

Inside, the temple smelled of sandalwood and jasmine. The sacred book lay beneath a richly-decorated canopy. The holy men read and chanted continuously and their voices sounded to Jazz like a strong wind blowing through leaves.

'All day they are reading from the holy book,' whispered Herjit. 'Any person may come in to take part.'

As each visitor left the temple, they were offered a spoonful of some special food, served from a huge dish directly into their open hands.

Jazz wasn't sure what it was. It was white, sticky and

sweet-tasting, like a marshmallow pudding.

'This is *prasad*,' said Harjit. 'A sort of present. They give it to make us welcome.'

The family found a low wall where they could sit together in the shade to eat their *prasad*.

Jazz remembered the story Mrs Macpherson read of how those three wise men travelled all that way to the stable taking offerings with them to make the newborn child welcome. Now it was like the other way round. The holy men at the temple gave an offering to their visitors.

Jazz glanced down the long row that was her Punjabi family, spread along the wall, enjoying *prasad* from their cupped hands. Dr Elspeth, away at the far end of the line next to Oldest Auntiji, smiled and winked at Jazz. Then she beckoned her to join them.

'I believe your Auntiji has something to show you,' she said, making room on the wall for Jazz. 'She was no too sure if you'd like it. But I said I thought you would.'

Oldest Auntiji mumbled as she fished about in the pocket of her tunic. She drew out a folded-up card. She placed it in Jazz's hand.

Jazz unfolded it carefully. She thought there must be something inside that would fall out. The card had been folded and unfolded so many times that the fold-lines had almost worn through. It was a photograph, very blurred, and repeated folding had rubbed off the print till the middle of the picture was hardly visible any more.

It had once been a photo of a young man. He was standing in front of a white decorated building in the middle of a pool. Jazz recognised it.

'It's here, isn't it?' she said. 'It's at the Golden Temple.'

The young man's face was almost entirely worn away by the fold-lines so you couldn't see if he was solemn or smiling.

'It's him, isn't it?' she said. 'He came here.' He must have been smiling. Jazz was sure he was.

'Auntiji said it was taken just before he left for Britain. He

94

sent it to her after he'd arrived in Glasgow.'

When Jazz handed it back Oldest Auntiji shook her head.

Dr Elspeth said, 'I think she'd like you to keep it.'

Jazz refolded it along the many creases and put it into her own pocket. 'Thank you, Auntiji.'

She could feel the most intense and wonderful pain breaking inside her, like a star that was bursting. She supposed that this might be what dying of a broken heart was like, except it felt all right.

'Will you tell her, Dr Elspeth, that it's the finest thing that's happened to me since I arrived.'

Jazz looked at the other families wandering peacefully beside the still water. She looked up at the doves fluttering and tumbling through the air, white birds against a deep blue sky.

Here, in such peace, nothing was scary. It might be bearable to think about the dangerous and difficult things you hadn't wanted to think about before.

Jazz wasn't sure if she was going back to Bridie or to the boring couple with the goldfish. She knew now she had to do what she could to hang on to Bridie, even if she didn't actually get to live with her. It was odd not knowing where you were next going to live, what the next stage of your life would be about. Yet somehow Jazz had a feeling she was going to be able to manage.

She hoped it was true, what Elspeth said, that you could belong to more than one place at once, that you didn't have to actually be there all the time, but were still a part of it. Then these aunties would still be her aunties even when she wasn't here.

Maybe, Jazz thought, when she grew up and got a job and grew rich, she could take Bridie travelling, to Galway one year, to the Punjab the next, for the rest of their lives.

Or maybe, even if she never got rich, never managed to bring Bridie here, she'd still be able to hold on to the memory and tell Bridie about it. And about the bald dog, and the new baby, and the funny toddlers, and sharing everything with Harjit and Surinder and Kuldeep and Pritpal, and the oldest Auntiji with sad eyes and worn-out hands.

And she could explain to Bridie that, even if Rajinder's people didn't believe in the same angels as Bridie did, her prayer had been answered and her own angels had been taking care of Jazz all the time.

'Come now, Sister,' said Harjit. 'Uncle is going to buy us fresh sweet lime-soda drinks.'

'Okay, Sis. Wait for me.'